Cindy —

JOURNEY TO
Jutrai

Enjoy every step
of your Journey —
thru life —

Lauri
Mason

ROBIN MOYER ～

JOURNEY TO Jukai

ROBIN MOYER

Wynwidyn PRESS
PINCKNEY, MI

ROBIN MOYER ～

Dedication

To my muses, Drew Barnhill and Robin Williams
~please know you will always be seen!

Robin

ROBIN MOYER ～

Moments While Traveling

Sunrise braiding

vermillion and saffron ribbons

of mare's tail clouds

across a sky washed blue with dawn.

A yellow jacket catches my eye

across a gloomy twist of snaking lines;

the only sting is not knowing who she is.

A ghost of a dream lingers

with sky braids holding hands with tomorrow.

Joshua (written on the plane)

ROBIN MOYER ～

Prologue

The Yūrei, formerly known as Minami, flickered in the deep darkness of the Forest of Jukai. Her blue-green flame brightened, revealing her limp-handed, white robed visage. She felt a strong pulling, a tugging that was leading her out of the dampness of the Suicide Forest also known as Aokigahara and to the east. She had never encountered anything like this before. Since her murder, she'd felt as if she were forbidden to leave this place where she'd 'awakened' after everything went dark. Yet now, suddenly, she felt that she was supposed to leave, as if some purpose hovered at the edge of her consciousness.

Minami felt herself pulled up and beyond Mount Fuji until she was wafting out over the Pacific, high above the waters writhing below. In life, she'd never left Japan, indeed, had never ventured far from the village where she had been born. Even when her father had sold her to the farmer a few miles away, that was as far as she had ever traveled.

She heard snatches of sound, of voices. Or, were they thoughts? She felt waves of pain wash over her, and yet, she recognized that the pain was not her own. The pulling was stronger now, and she glided east, through the night, and met the dawn of a new day.

Now, she was aware of what she had to do. She knew whom it was she needed to find; no, there were more than one. Mentally she shrugged, still not comprehending the why behind the urge; but she knew it was something she was supposed to do, to help. She needed to find them quickly, before it was too late. She needed to stop them; she needed to convince them. She had to somehow bring them home.

PART One : LUGGAGE

ROBIN MOYER

Chapter 1

Joshua sat up in bed, startled from uneasy sleep by a crash of thunder. Looking out his window at the lightning flashing around the bridge, he thought, *Today seems as good a day as any to kill myself.* He had been contemplating it for some time now, and while nothing specific had occurred to make it all gel at that precise moment, it never-the-less had done so, and he smiled his first real smile in several months.

It wasn't that his life was all that bad, actually. He had no life-threatening disease that would slowly sap him of energy. He had a job of sorts; nothing fancy, but it paid the rent on his studio apartment in San Francisco. Not even a bad studio, really, and it had a view of the bridge. He did not owe unborn children to debt collectors. Rationally, his life was pretty good. At least that's what everyone told him. What did they know?

They didn't know that from the second he woke up in the morning, until the time he was able to fall asleep at night, his mind whirled with thoughts. Sometimes they connected together, but at other times, they were a disjointed mish-mash of half-formed ideas, one following the other, overlapping or crashing together, oft times his thoughts spinning out of control like a crazed carousel. He couldn't focus for the kaleidoscope of images.

Thoughts, memories, photographic moments of possible artwork, like torn and shredded pieces of tissue paper, were 'decoupage-d' in his head, blurring or blocking complete thoughts, causing them to dam up until he sometimes felt his brain literally would ooze out of his ears.

They didn't know, couldn't know, because he'd never told anyone, that he felt completely, utterly, overwhelmingly inadequate. From his earliest memory, he had never been able to please his father. Nothing was ever clean enough, high enough, good enough, far enough for his father who always seemed to be perfect at everything, except understanding Joshua. 'Can't you do anything right?' was the refrain he heard over and over again.

He had never been able to keep up with his younger sports-star twin brothers. He'd never really wanted to; he didn't particularly even care to watch sports, let alone play them. He'd always wondered what the whole point of it was. Competition to see who could 'win?' Or be the least 'beat up?' Or get there (wherever 'there' was) first, fastest or cleanest? None of which mattered because, even if he had been interested, he still would have lagged behind Boy 1 and Boy 2 by a mile. He'd always referred to them in his head as Boy 1 and Boy 2; had ever since his folks had brought them home from the hospital and that's what the tags around their wrists said. More, his parents hadn't settled on names yet and he heard his father refer to them that way.

According to his father, at only a few days old, he could already tell that the twins were special. They had the looks, the brains and the brawn. Most people couldn't begin to tell Jason and Justin apart, but Josh always could. Jason's ears stuck out more. Josh was the first-born, but it had always seemed to him, and was what his parents implied, that he was created out of the cosmic leftovers no one else wanted, and the choicest bits were saved for Jason and Justin.

Even when his three sisters trickled along, he'd been unable to compete — relegated to the position of 'babysitter' because, again, according to his dad, he wasn't good for much else.

As they'd grown, he somehow had been lost in the shuffle, never measuring up and certainly never earning respect from anyone. The twins were smart, beautiful, popular and complete snobs. They aced college, married (as they'd been bred to do) lawyers and doctors, and each had two perfect children who were mini-images of their mothers. The corporate world had never interested him personally. Boy 1 and Boy 2 had, from day one, been the focal point (or points) of his parents' world and had eagerly followed the parental trail to business school and the eventual CEO status that they believed they so richly deserved.

He, on the other hand, felt lost in their world, but happiest when creating something, anything. He wrote, painted, sculpted, played the piano and composed music. He turned their garden into an award winning English Garden, for which his mother took complete credit in her gracious acceptance speech. It simply did not matter what he did. When he won an award for 'best new artist' or received a ribbon for poetry in school, his father would grouse to anyone within hearing that, 'It was a total waste of time as, Lord knows, the boy never will make a living slopping paint on a canvas or words on a page.'

He had moved out the day their world had fallen apart. Not so much because of the collapse, but because, in the midst of the chaos, he could. And did. Initially, no one even realized he'd left. Eventually they did, at which point he was long gone.

He'd always felt as though the day the towers fell was his independence day. When he saw the first images on the TV, Josh knew there was no way his father possibly could survive. He would have been at his business meeting on the 89th floor. There could be no way his father could get out of that. Then, later, as first one, then the second tower fell, everyone knew. Not even 'Indestructo,' as Boys 1 and 2 referred to their dad, could stand up to tons of concrete and steel.

Josh had stuffed his clothes into a duffle, his notebooks and brushes into a backpack. He did it knowing he could always get more paint, but he particularly liked those brushes. Looking around his room one last time, he reached over and grabbed a dog-eared book on painting that was his 'go to' book for techniques. *Can't leave that behind,* he'd thought. *It's what got me painting in the first place.* Josh shook his head as he closed the door behind him. *Pretty sad that I can pack my life into two bags.*

He hadn't gone far, didn't really feel the need to: he just needed to be in his own place, his own space. In the ten years or so that he'd been out on his own, he'd gotten by with art gigs or freelance writing for one of the numerous rags that spewed forth from almost every corner of Frisco. He'd had a few showings, but nothing much had happened as a result of them. Sure, he'd sold a few pieces, but never quite felt as if he'd 'made it.' He just didn't seem to get along well with the 'right' people and was brutally inept at playing the games one always had to play.

He'd met Susi at the coffee house down the street and they'd hung out together for a couple of years. He'd never felt that he was in love with her, certainly nothing near what she claimed to feel for him. However, it had been comfortable and familiar and she'd gotten it when he was in write-mode or paint-mode and left him alone. They were like a comfortable old sweater, worn until the elbows needed patching and both the pockets were full of holes.

That was until her body's alarm clock started going off and she started bugging him about kids. Kids? He still felt like one himself. If he wasn't 'grown up', how could he take care of a kid that needed him to be a parent? He had told Susi that he would be a rotten parent and she should find someone who would be good at that sort of stuff. She'd nodded, packed her stuff and walked out without another word. So much for two years' of Susi. All things considered, he'd actually been more invested in her than she'd been in him to just walk away. And, as the Susi habit had quickly faded, he guessed he hadn't been all that invested either.

Things hadn't been too bad until he'd hit a wall three months ago. That's when he'd heard that his mom was dying of cancer about a week before she actually did.

She'd stopped by on her way home from the doctor's office. Although she'd been sick for some time now, she hadn't wanted the family to know and worry. There was no changing the inevitable, and she knew it, she'd told him. She'd said she should have come by more often. She apologized for not being more on his side growing up.

Making her peace, he thought, letting her ramble. Polluted water under the bridge as far as he was concerned, but he loved her none the less and attempted to make her feel better. She left with a smile and a hug and seemed to be in a better frame of mind. It was what it was. He could no more change her road than he could change the past. He thought about one more trip to the house (it wasn't and hadn't been home for long before he'd left) but decided that his private time with his mom had been their goodbye and nothing else needed to be said, especially not within radar range of the sibling artillery.

A week later he received the phone call that she'd passed away in her sleep.

The sisters all came with their numerous offspring. They did all the fussing, cooking and crying that accompany a death in the family. It had seemed so scripted to Josh and, while he'd never been close to his mother, what he saw in that empty house just didn't feel like grief or sorrow to him. His brothers came, each with a wife and set of twins to add to the kid noise and swagger. Boys 1 and 2 drank his mother's bar dry, pontificated on the price they'd get for the house, dressed perfectly for the funeral and then blew sky high at the reading of the will.

Back after he'd first moved out, his mother had called asking if there was anything of his dad's that he wanted. There hadn't been and she'd said she'd let the rest of the family divvy it up. So now, it was all Mom-stuff. The long paid-off house would be sold and the money for it would go to Josh. There were trusts set up for all the grandchildren for college. But since, according to the will, the twins and the girls were all set money-wise, his mother figured she 'owed' it to Josh.

"Not me or Jason? Not Sara Beth, Tracey Ann or Lilly Dawn? Not to the grandkids? Mom's leaving it all to the black sheep, the 'do nothing', useless son who never accomplished anything at all, to the total loser?" Josh could still hear in his mind's ear his brothers' raging tantrums. His family, if one could call them that, walked out *en masse* and that was the last he'd heard from them personally. Their assorted lawyers had contacted the family attorney and tried to break the will, but in that, they had failed, individually and collectively.

The house sold for a fraction of what it was once worth. With the economy the way it was, he was lucky, he figured, to get anything. When the medical bills were paid, the family lawyer paid off and the papers signed, he'd received just under fifteen grand. He stuck it in the bank and figured it was a good emergency fund. Though, what sort of emergency was left was beyond him. He didn't have a car or a girlfriend and didn't owe much of anything to anyone. No one seemed to get it and they probably never would; he didn't care about the blood money. His *family* could have fought over their thirty pieces of silver and he had actually thought about telling the lawyers to let them have it. He grinned. It was more fun this way.

It was then he'd gotten a letter from one Jonathan M. Reicliff, Esq. His grandmother Alice had passed away the previous year. He didn't remember her at all, aside from a few hazy half-formed images from when he was very young. What vague memory persisted was colored by veiled comments and unanswered questions when Christmas and birthday presents would arrive.

According to the attorney's letter, she'd left a considerable amount to him, a house and funds to keep it going to another relative, an undisclosed sum to yet a third relative, exactly which relatives, according to the attorney, was not to be disclosed to him, and the rest of her estate had been left to her cat, of all things.

Between the two inheritances, he had no money issues for the near or (for that matter) far future. That should have made him feel happy, but it didn't do much more than leave him more confused than ever, with more questions than ever and no source from which he might get some answers. Eventually, a package arrived from the attorney's office containing several of his grand-mother's journals. Checking dates, he knew he had not received *all* of the journals for some reason. He, then, had spent the last two months reading years of his grandmother's journal entries. What world he had, had been rocked out from under him. Before, he was a screwed up mess; now, he was a confused, rich screwed up mess. *Hell of an inheritance!*

The truths within Grandma Alice's writings turned him inside out. He was left wondering if anything he'd grown up with was real. His father wasn't his father at all. While it explained a lot, it raised more questions that he had no answers for, nor anyone left to ask. Who was his real father? What had happened to him? Did he even know Josh existed? Who walked away from whom? Had his mother told his dad, well, his stepdad, the truth or did he think Josh was his and the gene pool had been empty that day? Why had no one ever told *him?* Both the twins and the girls looked like their dad in some ways, but Josh had been all his mother. Well, except for his eyes. Joshua's eyes were a startling deep leafy green. Algae eyes, Boy 1 always called them. Nevertheless, his 'parents' (for lack of a better word) had had blue eyes, as did his brothers and sisters.

That truth had been only the first of numerous startling truths. That his grandmother had not wanted his mother to marry his 'dad' was another, but she was pregnant and in their society, one did not get pregnant outside of marriage. Playing with dates, he realized that his parents had been married when she was a few months pregnant with the twins and he would have been, what?

Three? Why did he not know that? Did his siblings know? Or did everyone know but him? What else didn't he know? Did his folks want to avoid Grandma or had she avoided them?

As he continued to read the journals, he realized that his mother had gone out of her way to avoid his stepdad's mother, although from what his grandmother wrote, his 'dad' didn't have much of a problem with it. Eventually he read that his grandmother had wanted him to know the truth about who he was and how it wasn't his fault that his 'dad' had never treated him the same way he had the rest of the kids.

Didn't do him much good now, he thought. Had she expected him to blithely discard twenty plus years of conditioning, of molding, or perhaps did she look for the resolute breaking of the enforced molding? It wasn't as if everything that he'd been told, as if everything he'd felt could be cast off like an unwanted jacket or washed out of him like paint from a brush.

Not only was he not who they tried to make him into, he wasn't even who he thought he was. Which left him wondering who he was at all.

One passage from his Grandmother's journals stuck in his mind. She'd written so matter-of-factly about it.

"I do not know why Justin married Laura. To take on another woman's child is so unlike him. It might work for some men, but never Justin. I feel badly for the boy. He'll never be good enough in Justin's eyes."

He'd stared at himself in the chipped mirror he'd picked up at the consignment shop down the block. Tawny, sun-streaked hair curled long to his shoulders. Green eyes with flecks of gold like a starburst around his pupils, Mossy green he liked to think, that always seemed fathomless. Susi used to say she felt as if she could fall into them. Flat, thin, brown eyebrows, a straight nose, a wide smile and orthodontically perfect teeth reflected back at him. Same old face he'd grown up with, and now, that of a total stranger. He'd never fit in because he was from a different set.

He'd been the puzzle piece that someone had broken trying to jam it in place when it was the wrong size, the wrong shape and from a completely different picture. It was then that his hand, fisted so hard at his side that his nails cut into his palm, flashed up and out, smashing the mirror, splintering his image into disjointed shards.

That was when he realized that he was lost. It was if he had some sort of identity amnesia; he knew who he was but he had no clue who he *was*. Caught in the midst of half-truths, lies and omissions, little made sense. Nothing felt real or honest.

Then, it got worse. Nothing he painted, when he managed to come up with a wisp of an idea, came even close to what he saw in his mind's eye. As if that hadn't been bad enough, he couldn't write either. Words fell lifelessly on the page. Meaning dribbled away like a bottle of spilled ink. He needed to write or paint. Both were his air and his blood; but he could do neither and it was killing him.

He'd thought about ending it all so many times. He'd thought about the how. He knew he couldn't blow his head off. That idea made his stomach hurt. Besides, who'd be stuck cleaning up the mess?

The bridge called to him. It always had. The idea of falling didn't bother him. It was like a final flight to freedom. It was clean and he'd simply just wash away in the waters below the bridge. It appealed to the writer in him; the symbolism of the bridge itself. It would be a link between the hell in his head and the heaven of peace. It wasn't so much about the wanting to die, really. He just couldn't live with everything the way it was now.

He'd thought about if he should leave a note, and if so, to whom? What could he say that would explain the unexplainable? He'd had a brief image of his brothers laughing over it, and that decided it for him. No note. No one needed to know why he did what he did. There was no one out there who deserved to under- stand because there was no one out there who would. Or could.

It was still raining when Joshua walked up onto the pedestrian walkway of the Golden Gate Bridge. He'd been fascinated by the bridge most of his life. It seemed to draw him to itself, and he'd spent endless hours painting it. He knew it was the number one spot in the entire world for committing suicide. Of course, you couldn't spend any time at all in San Francisco and not know this. Every time there was another suicide, that fact and the current state of the 'net the bridge' controversy was brought up yet again.

The area of the bridge, long before the bridge was conceived, indeed, even before gold was discovered in California, was from John Fremont's memoirs. In them, in 1846, Fremont wrote, "To this Gate I gave the name of 'Chrysopylae,' or 'Golden Gate,' for the same reasons that the harbor of Byzantium was called Chrysoceras, or 'Golden Horn.' " In fact, Joshua was listening to *Chrysopylae Reflections,* by James Kellaris, as he walked the bridge. First performed just this past spring as the 75th Anniversary theme, the music, too, spoke to him and was an oft-played choice on his iPhone. Joshua stood, leaning against the side of the bridge. The music on his iPhone had sputtered to a stop as his battery died. It didn't matter, he thought. Nothing much did, now. He just needed to shut his brain down. But the words, words that for months wouldn't come, began to move. He remembered a verse from Joseph Strauss' poem:

> *Launched midst a thousand hopes and fears,*
> *Damned by a thousand hostile sneers,*
> *Yet ne'er its course was stayed,*
> *But ask of those who met the foe*
> *Who stood alone when faith was low,*
> *Ask them the price they paid.*

He'd always particularly liked that verse. Still, his mind wouldn't stop. He noticed how the raindrops fell, sliding, falling down along the cables, red-orange tears; today, even the bridge was crying. *Now poetic words spew forth? Now?* A couple passed behind him arguing over money one or the other had spent. It was noise, background noise, irritating in that it was drowning out the echoes of the music on his phone. Stupid battery picking then to die on him.

The water seventy-five feet below looked November cold, waves flattened against the rain slashing down. He was thoroughly soaked, not that it mattered. The sky was a roiling mass of clouds as he looked out over the bay. He wished they'd built the walking path on the ocean side. He liked looking out to the nothingness beyond – rather than at the hills and homes and city beyond clustered on the brink of the bay, looking for all the world as if they, too, wanted to just let it all fly free and jump.

Enough, he told himself. Looking both ways over his shoulders, he started to climb over the cable to the ledge below.

"You cannot do this here. You cannot do this now."

"What? Where?" Josh looked around, but there was no one standing nearby. In fact, there was no one anywhere in sight. Even the car lanes were empty.

"You cannot do this here. You cannot do this now," repeated the voice, this time sounding feminine.

Josh whipped his head around to his other side. Nothing. "Don't tell me what I can or cannot do. Go away!"

"I must and you, must not. Not here. Not now."

Looking out over the water, Josh once again tried to climb over the cable. It was if there were a clear, glass wall between him and the ledge, between him and the water. He punched his fist out and it collided with an unseen surface he knew was not there.

Then, hovering just out of reach, he saw a white blur. After a moment, and after he had stepped back away from the railing, it became more focused. A woman, with long black hair, mussed and wind-blown, floated before him. She wore a long white kimono and did not appear to have any feet, for the bottom of it blew freely in the wind as if she had but half a body. Her arms, down to her elbows were at her sides, but her forearms reached out to him, although her hands hung limply from her wrists. On either side of her, two bluish-green flames flickered faintly.

"What, who are you?"

"It matters not, but I am a Yūrei."

"Well, go away."

"You cannot do this here. You cannot do this now. If you truly wish to die, if you truly wish to commit suicide, then you must journey to Aokigahara. You must go to Jukai."

"Journey to Aokiga-what?"

"You must journey to Aokigahara first. Then, and only then can you make the right choice for yourself. My time here is short. Do not tell anyone of this. Just remember, you must journey to Aokigahara."

"Like anyone would believe me anyway! They would think I was crazy."

"And preparing to jump off a bridge is not? Go to Jukai, Joshua." With these words, she faded away, leaving the two bluish-green flames to blink out behind her.

Joshua shook his head, as if to clear his thoughts. Then, determined, once again, he tried to climb over the railing. He still could not get past the invisible barrier. Defeated, he turned and saw that once again, the bridge was full of rush hour traffic and people were walking under umbrellas along the walkway. One of the bridge security cops was eying him warily.

Okay, not here, not now. But soon, and where, and when I choose!

Chapter 2

Emily sat, curled within herself, on the top step of the attic stairs in her grandmother's house. Her house, really, but it still felt like her grandmother's home. Up here, it seemed as if she could still smell her grandmother's perfume, Estée Lauder's 'Youth Dew.' The old wallpaper lining the attic stairwell seemed infused with it, as if the floral rosebud pattern would release it as she brushed by.

Even from here, she could clearly hear the argument going on two floors below. Her parents were having yet another of their constant arguments: loud, vicious, and, as usual, over her. Well, specifically over her current state of uselessness, the fact that she never finished anything she started and the fact that once again she was under their roof and not contributing a damn thing.

That, at least, from what she was able to gather, was her father's take. Stepfather, really, she reminded herself. Of course, her mother had never liked the term and had insisted Emily refer to him as 'father.' She'd never really known her real dad; she'd been only two when he died. All she had were fuzzy memories of someone tall who'd tossed her laughing in the air. Emily figured she must have been three or four when her mother had found Nick, and from then on, it was if her real dad ceased to exist; had never existed. She had vague memories of pictures of him being scattered about, but after Nick came on the scene, they'd vanished, and she'd never seen them again.

The trouble began back when she'd been little and her mother realized that, due to difficulties birthing Emily, she hadn't been able to carry another child. For some reason, Nick had always blamed this on Emily too.

The yelling was all Nick now. Her mother had stopped defending Emily and switched into what Emily always thought of as her mother's 'calm him down before anything happens' mode.

Biting her lip, Emily thought about how Grandma Alice had left the house to her, not her parents. Thoughts swirled about her *inability,* as her father had so delicately phrased it, to finish anything. No, she hadn't finished her photography course. No, she hadn't stayed in college and, most recently, no, she hadn't carried through on a pregnancy she was ill prepared to handle.

That, of course, was the funny part. Nick had blasted her for being so stupid to get pregnant in the first place. Then, when he found out about the abortion, he'd absolutely lost it; screaming at her about the fires of hell, for never, ever, finishing anything and for being so selfish to take a life that wasn't hers to take.

Where was her mother's advice and support now? Her mom had agreed it was for the best and Emily had known she'd never have been able to give it up for adoption had she had the baby. Her ex-boyfriend, he being the one who had vanished immediately after her joyful announcement, was no help either. She'd known she had no way to raise a child by herself and her step-dad had made it blatantly clear he wouldn't help her.

Sometimes, it didn't seem to matter what she did or didn't do. Whatever choice she made was wrong. Her dad had flat out hated Larry, calling him a no-good bum, but when she told her parents that he had left her, suddenly it was her fault. She'd told him about the baby in the wrong way; she'd tried to trap the poor boy.

Emily's long russet brown hair dusted the steps below her as she cradled her head on her arms. She'd wanted the baby. She'd have had someone that was all hers, someone to love who would love her back. The morning after, she felt as if she were dying: As if the child was haunting her, condemning her. *As well it should,* she thought now. *She'd been so wrong. Who cared if it was legal? She'd taken a life with no good reason, and that thought was killing her, bit by bit, every day.*

Ever since her grandmother had passed away a year ago, she really felt as if she had no one. The house, and the trust fund to maintain it, was hers, of course, but it wasn't enough to raise a child. Sure, she had her monthly spending stipend, which, all things being said, was more than adequate, but she could not have raised a child here and, without the house, there was no money.

Downstairs, the voices raised yet another notch on the screaming scale. From her spot on the top step, the current argument below now focused on her father resenting that the house and the funds to keep it going were left to Emily rather than her mother.

"Why'd your damn mother leave it to her anyway? Where does she get off saying that we can't touch the funds to keep it going? I've never understood why the old bat gave her total control anyway. It makes no sense."

"You know she wanted Emily to have something to fall back on."

"Yeah, because she can't do a damn thing right. I tell ya, Lizzie, sometimes I think you gave the wrong---"

"Nick! Don't say it."

"Well, we need to find a way to break that trust. She was your mother, you need to find a way or get your kid to sign it over to us. And the cat! She leaves the rest to the damn cat! Emily, come downstairs," he yelled. *Not happening, Father,* Emily thought. *I'm not stupid. It is bad enough that when I came back home you'd kicked me out of my own room and tossed my stuff in the attic. It's bad enough that you and mom took over my room. You are not getting control of this house. You may control her, but you will not control me.*

"Emily!" Her father's voice echoed up the stairs. "Get down here this minute. NOW!" His voice got even louder, as if half the neighborhood couldn't already hear him, as if she were stone deaf that she hadn't been able to hear every cold word he'd uttered.

Emily stood up, went the rest of the way up into her room, closed the door and locked it. She grabbed her cell and her back-pack, opened the French doors that lead out onto a small porch and stepped outside. Slinging on her backpack, she carefully climbed over the edge of the balcony and stepped onto the branch of the maple tree outside her room. Shinnying down between the branches, she dropped from the last branch and headed down the street.

She hadn't made it two blocks when she was grabbed from behind and spun around. Nick stood there, his face red from chasing after her. "Where the hell do you think you're going? I didn't say you could leave. Get back to the house now." He pointed down the street.

Emily didn't move. "If you know what's good for you, you will go back to the house now. Or," he paused, glaring at her, his eyes hooded, his lips pursed, "do I need to drag you?"

Knowing he'd likely do just that, she shook her head. Her shoulders slumping in dejection, she walked back to the house. He walked alongside her, his hand hard as he held her arm firmly. "Your mother needs you. She fell in the kitchen."

"What?" Emily looked up at him. "Did you hit her again, you son of a – "She took off running for the house. Going down the path to the back door, she took the short flight of steps two at a time. She skidded to a stop seeing her mother sitting on the kitchen floor, her eye already swelling shut. Reaching for the freezer door, Emily flung it open and grabbed the first bag of frozen vegetables her hand touched.

"Mom," she said handing them to her mother, "Mom, why do you let him do this to you?"

Lizzie, her mother, just tilted her head, her one good eye looking at Emily. "You know how he gets. It is your fault. He went up to get you and found your door locked. After he kicked it in and realized you were gone, he came down here and the swinging door from the living room hit me as he came back into the kitchen."

"No it didn't. He hit you. Again."

"You want to talk about hitting?" Nick came in through the kitchen door, his fist already mid-swing. He connected with the side of her head, knocking her into the kitchen table. "That's what you get for not doing what I say. This is what you get for acting so all high and mighty with this being *your* house! I live here. It will be our house, not yours. Do you hear me? You will do what needs to be done, sign what needs signing, but you will make this house mine, or else. "

More blows had accompanied each statement. When she'd slid under the table, he'd simply knocked it across the room. Tears streamed down her face, her head aching from the numerous blows, she curled into a defensive ball.

Nick grabbed her hair and pulled her to a standing position. He opened the door and shoved her outside. "You go now. You are not getting back in this house until you have paperwork deeding it to your mother and me. Don't you so much as dare get all in a huff about how your grandmother left it to you. Our lawyer will prove that she was batty when she died and make sure we get it. In addition, I'll get you locked up for being crazy. How'd you like that? We've always known you were not all there in the head."

Although he'd shoved her out the door, he hadn't let go of her arm. "Yeah, never mind, you ain't going nowhere except the loony bin. I'll get you committed and then get it all nice and legal-like and you'll have no choice. I'll tell them you beat the shit outta your mother, that's what I'll do, and don't you worry none, she will do whatever I say, won't ya Lizzie? How'd ya like them apples, baby?"

Emily tore her arm out of his hand and took off running down the block. She ducked down the second alleyway, hopped over Miss Abby's back fence and ran across her back yard. Down at the back, she pushed through the late autumn roses, scratching her face as she did so, and squeezed through the loose boards at the edge of the property. Still running, she skirted round the edge of the schoolyard and headed for the park. Behind her, she could hear both Nick screaming and the sound of an approaching siren. *Good,* she thought, *maybe someone finally called the cops on him.*

Several hours later, she sat hunkered down in Captain P's, her favorite pub down near the marina. Somehow, she'd managed to keep her backpack on and so she had her laptop with her. Taking advantage of the local Wi-Fi, she opened her Gmail account and saw a new email from her friend, Amy, who lived across the street. Surprised to be getting an email from her, as they really hadn't been close since high school, she clicked it open.

Em, what the hell's going on at your house? Tried calling ya, but your phone went to VM. Cops came, then the ambulance. They took your mom to the hospital and your dad left in the back of a cop car. I could hear him screaming and cussing all the way over here about how you beat the shit out of your mom!!!! He was saying you went nuts and threatened to kill them both. As if! I heard the cops say they were looking for you for questioning or something, though. Don't know where you went, but I thought you'd want to know what's going on. Later, Amy

She sat there staring at the email. *Answer it...or not?* Emily wished she'd grabbed her phone before she left. *Do I dare go back to the house? Should I? Who would the cops believe? What should I do?*

Chapter 3

That moment in time when she was ready to leap – when she had to wait patiently for the air to catch the sail of the glider just right – that was one of the moments she savored. There was just something about that space of time, balanced at the edge of forever, when it all came down to taking that step into nothingness where, if the fates didn't align, she would be stepping into her own demise.

The adrenaline rush, the anticipation, the thrill: Jinn lived for those moments, for indeed, it was in the space of those moments when she felt most alive. She looked out over the waters of the North Sea. The water was a deep blue today; the tips of the waves frothed and foamed as they crashed into themselves. For a brief moment, she looked down, down beyond her feet clinging to the very edge of the granite cliff. Far, far below, the waves toyed with the boulders lining the base. The air curled under, she felt the tug and rising to her toes, she leapt off the edge of the cliff . . .

Jinn caught the wave of air rising up from the sea below. It pushed her up and out where she could catch the air current as it rose higher still; the air, warm from the reflected heat off the baked, dried soil, carried her on. She coasted out over the ocean, high enough now that the cliff seemed a remote entity. She knew better, than to glide so close to the cliffs, but the air felt so glorious, the rush of it as she rose higher, and the sheer silence as she circled round in a long, lazy oval to glide along the very edge of them. Close to the towering granite walls, using the heated air pushing off the black rocks, she flew, startling seabirds that scaled away and down.

A heartbeat later, caught by a downdraft, a miscalculation of wind and air, and she'd lost control. The glider lost elevation, spiraled and fell. Even as she'd tried to correct, even as the foamed rocks below loomed larger, even as the rescue boats whistled their alerts, the thought crossed Jinn's mind that this was 'living on the edge.' Bringing the glider out of the stall just before she hit the waves, she flattened her approach and settled into the water with a splash.

Jinn wandered aimlessly down the cobblestone street in San Francisco. She'd been back from Scotland for a few weeks now, and, frankly, she was going out of her mind. She'd left Scotland because she was bored. She'd done the castle thing, couldn't understand a word people said to her, and her traveling partner, Jeff, had decided to stay in Scotland for a few extra weeks to play golf at St. Andrews. Golf? How staid and dull! Even if it *was* a game played where golf had been born. *Extreme sports, hah! Golf was extreme boring.*

They'd traveled to Scotland to take part in the Series 4 cliff jumps near Black Hill. These were flights made with a para-glider and then measured by height, airtime and distance. Jeff'd never gotten his chance to jump, thanks to her ill-timed flight that had ended up with both the glider and her bobbing around in the North Sea. That's what she got for wanting to get in close, to skirt the rim. Yet even as she'd been going down, she had relished the free falling, the weightlessness of it, as if she had been flying.

She'd barely missed the truck-sized boulders lining the edge of the cliff. Then according to the medics, she'd almost been suffering hypothermia by the time the save-boat maneuvered close enough to fish her out. Three men had leapt into the choppy waves to assist her. But she'd just felt warm and pumped. Everyone had made such a fuss over how close she'd come to being dashed on the rocks, but Jinn just had laughed it off. Jinn knew the risks they took, but that was a major part of the thrill.

Wrapped in a woolen blanket, she was still thinking about the sight of sun glinting off the wet rocks, glittering sparkles on grey and black and the water foaming and spewing from between the granite that formed the cliffs. The droplets of water catching the sun transformed them into shiny diamonds and the lure was inescapable.

The thrill. It was like caffeine is to most folks, Jinn mused. It was a natural high that got her blood moving; an adrenaline rush like no other. It made her feel alive. As if she was simply more than she was normally, even if Jeff thought she was addicted to it. *So what?* She could think of worse things to be addicted to. Remembering back to the fight they'd had a week ago, just before Jeff took off to go play golf and she'd decided to head back to the states alone, Jinn could still hear the recrimination in his voice.

"One of these days you will take a thoughtless risk and kill yourself. Do you have a death wish? I don't, and I won't stick around and watch you die. Did you even thank the men who went in after you? It is always about you and experiencing the thrill, isn't it? There is more to life than that, Jinn!"

Running her fingers through her wind-tousled and sunstreaked mahogany hair, Jinn brushed her bangs out of her eyes. Deep blue eyes, the color of the North Sea, Jeff had told her. Right. She bet his were greener than the greens where he was off knocking a little white ball around with a club. Where's the thrill in that? She hoped he got lots of, what were they called? Birdies. She felt like giving him a bird or three. She didn't understand his whole attitude of late. He was the one who had gotten her into paragliding, bungee jumping and free falling in the first place. A bit late for him to decide he was a wuss. Who was he to say she took unnecessary risks. Wasn't that the point? Darn Jeff anyway.

She just needed to find something new to do. She'd done the paragliding thing now, bungee-jumped, cliff dove in Mexico...skiing maybe? She needed that edge, that rush. Maybe she'd head south and go surfing. Yeah, the weather was good and she'd heard the waves had been good lately. She could go to Trestles or El Capitan, both of which were for experienced surfers and offered dangerous waves and breaks. Even though she knew just enough to fake it, the rides at both beaches were killers.

Jinn checked the surf conditions on her iPhone. No, maybe not such good waves. She sighed.

Wandering down the street, skirting little wrought-iron tables outside the numerous little cafes, she paused as a painting in a boutique gallery caught her eye. The Golden Gate Bridge at sunset. Living in San Francisco, the picture was by no means anything unusual. Seemed as if every painter had to put his spin on the iconic bridge, but there was something about this one, something different.

Stepping into the brightly lit gallery, Jinn went up to the painting. Done in watercolors, it seemed overly vibrant for the medium. The combination of inks and color seemed to make the bridge shimmer in the washes of sunset colors. It made the bridge almost vibrate off the paper. The artist had clouds of mist surrounding the edges of the bridge and it was if it floated, unattached to either shore – as if it could just waft elsewhere or something. Usually immune to paintings of the bridge, this one pulled at her. She glanced at the subtle tag tucked in the edge of the frame. The painting seemed woefully underpriced. She excused herself to step around a young man between her and the counter and waited for the mid-fifties woman dressed in a somber gray suit with a petal pink silk blouse to notice her.

The woman was talking with a gentleman dressed in a pinstriped suit. She could just overhear them talking about some of the paintings and then heard him reference the painting she intended to buy.

"He shows a deft touch for someone so young, but it doesn't offer the depth of vision that it should. It will be interesting to see his work if or when he reaches his potential."

Hah! Jinn thought. *A lot you know. The painting is magical and in this city, it is damn near impossible to find a painting of the bridge that truly looks different.*

Jinn paid for the painting and arranged to have it shipped to her house. Stepping back through the gallery, she noticed that the sad looking young man was silently staring at the now empty easel where the painting had been. *Snooze, you lose, bub,* she thought as she breezed out of the store.

Grabbing a latte at the next barista, she sat on a painted white wooden chair at a table created out of old apple crates. It was close to the trunk of a mimosa tree, and the feathery leaves cut just enough of the bright afternoon sun. The thrill of her artistic find had already vanished. She needed to do something. A blinking light on her phone caught her eye. New email. *Oh,* she thought. *More junk mail hitting her Gmail account. Hmm, cruise up-date.* She clicked open the email and saw an up to date listing of cruises leaving from LA, San Francisco and San Diego in the next few weeks. Jinn read down a list. Hawaii, New Zealand, Japan. *Hmmm.* She'd never been to Japan. *Kimonos were cool. Did they eat with chopsticks there, or was that China?* Jinn smiled at herself and clicked the link.

Chapter 4

Emily heard someone approaching her table. She looked up to see a police officer standing there.

"Miss Bridgewater? Miss Emily Bridgewater?"

"Y-yes, sir."

"I am Officer Davidson. We've been trying to find you. Do you know your mother is in the hospital? We picked up your stepfather earlier when we transported your mom. We need you to come down to the station and fill out a report about the incident this afternoon, please. Will you come with me?"

"Can't I just tell you here? Is my mom okay? I should go see her. What hospital?"

"No, miss. I need to take you downtown. Shouldn't take too long. We have statements from the neighbors and your mom filled in some of the holes. I see you've got quite the black eye. We will need pictures of that. You should get it looked at when you go see your mother. She's at St Joe's and she will be fine."

Emily's hand rose to her cheek. "It's okay, I mean, I'm okay. So this should be quick, right? I, um, won't have to see Nick, will I?" She powered down her laptop and put it in her backpack. She took one last sip of her coffee and stood up.

"No, miss. Not if you don't want to. It is just that he made certain accusations and we need to clear up any questions. After seeing you and your mother, I'd say it is a safe bet that your side of the story will be quite different from his.

Down at the station, the officer shepherded Emily into a small conference room.

"Please have a seat, an officer will be with you shortly," instructed Officer Davidson.

A small conference table and four chairs were placed in the middle of a sea-foam green room with an old cracked linoleum floor. Opposite the door was a wide, wall-sized mirror. A fluorescent light that buzzed annoyingly lighted the room.

Officer Cassiday, a female officer on the wrong side of thirty-five, paused briefly outside the conference room. Looking through the one-sided window into the room, she observed the twenty-five year old Emily for a moment. Dark brown hair with reddish highlights framed a heart-shaped face with startling blue eyes. An almost pretty little thing, but for her mouth, which seemed a bit too wide, and the beginnings of one heck of a shiner that currently had her left cheek swelling rapidly. She stood in the far corner beyond the table and seemed to be favoring her left arm, which she held cradled in her right hand. The officer opened the door and strode in.

"Hi. I'm Officer Cassiday. You are Emily Bridgewater, correct?"

"Yes, Ma'am."

"Have a seat, Emily. For your protection I must read you your Miranda Rights. You have the right to remain silent. Anything you say can be used against you in a court of law. You have the right to consult with a lawyer and have that lawyer present during the interrogation. If you cannot afford a lawyer, one will be appointed to represent you: Do you understand your rights as I have read them to you?"

"Yes, Ma'am. Interrogation? Am I under arrest?"

"No, not at this time, but I need you to tell me what happened today."

Emily explained about the argument she'd overheard, about her step-father being mad about the house, about her leaving and then being told and forced to leave again after he'd hit both her and her mother. She was trying to explain why he was so mad, but it was a long story and she didn't want to go into all the details.

"So, Emily, did you see Nick Fastello hit your mother?"

"No. She was on the floor when I got back to the house. She said the door had hit her when Nick ran back into the kitchen, but I didn't believe her. She always says she tripped or fell or slipped. She always has some excuse."

"Did you see either of them with a knife?"

"What knife? When? Who? Nick? Mom was just about barely able to sit up. Her eye was swelling shut. I got a bag of frozen veg-etables out of the freezer. Then Nick got back inside, hit me and told me to leave, but he wouldn't let go of my arm." Emily was crying now.

"He said he'd have me committed. He said he'd tell everyone I was crazy and if I was committed they they'd get my house. What knife?" she repeated, her voice rising. "Is my mom okay? Did he… oh God…did he…?

"Your mother will be okay. She lost some blood and will need some stiches, but she's okay. She's conscious and told me that Nick was waving the knife around and she got in the way."

"She always covers for him. Always has. It didn't used to be so bad, but it got worse after my grandmother died a year ago and left the house to me. He thought Grams should have left it to mom. I left to go take a photography course abroad and when I came back home unexpectedly, they'd just moved in, put all my stuff in the attic and took over my room."

"You'd been living on your own then?"

"Yes, ever since college. I was glad to have my own place, alone. He was always on my case how I should take care of them, how ungrateful I was for all they'd done for me. He'd show up at night without mom and yell at me, accuse me of abandoning her, them. I came back from a trip to the UK and there they both were; they'd completely moved in, changed the locks and said that it would be *unnatural* not to let them stay. No one would think anything of it. I *should* be the good child and do the right thing.

"So … where is Nick?" Emily looked around, looking towards the mirrored window.

"He's in a room down the hall giving his statement. I need to ask you a question. Do you want to press charges? Your mother refused."

Em shook her head. "Mom would never press charges. Not even when he broke her arm. She said she fell over the ottoman in the living room, but I know better. "

"Well," Officer Cassiday looked at Emily, flashing blue eyes meeting the officer's silver-grey, "what about you?"

"I – I don't know. I don't know what he'd do to me if I did. Or to Mom."

"Chances are, given you and your mother's testimony, he'd be doing some time. You'd have time to make arrangements. You can get a protection order against him."

Emily sighed. "Mom would just let him back and I can't kick my mom out on the street. I don't know what to do."

"Okay, well, we are going to keep him for a bit at any rate. He swung on one of the officers, so we've got him on that. You can go now and go see your mother. She'll be okay. And you need to be checked over as well."

Officer Cassiday walked Emily down the hallway. At a windowed counter, Emily signed the typed up statement. She saw Officer Davidson coming up the hallway.

"Are you ready to go now? I can bring you home or drop you off at the hospital."

"The hospital, please."

Chapter 5

Joshua sat in the dusk-shadowed room and watched a movie about Aokigahara on his computer. Outside, the sun sank in a blood red swath of color beyond the Golden Gate Bridge. On the screen, he watched as the narrator walked through the twisted trees of the forest Jukai where hundreds of people committed suicide every year.

He shivered. *Sure is a creepy place,* he mused. *Why should I have to go there? I have absolutely no desire to travel to Japan, of all places. I don't want to go anywhere. I'm too tired.*

Taking the bottle of pills he picked up at the pharmacy this morning, he turned it over and over in his hands. The outside of the bottle had numerous warnings against driving, overdosing, or taking on an empty stomach. Another warning said it could make him drowsy. *God only knew what the small print on the flier said.* He never bothered to read them anymore; not since one had said that it could cause suicidal thoughts, yet the doctors said the pills would keep him calm and stave off anxiety attacks. They would help him focus. *The marvels of modern medicine.*

I wonder how many it would take, he considered. The prescription was for sixty pills; one pill two times a day for thirty days. *I'm suicidal and they give me enough pills to kill myself.*

How wrong is that? He tried to open the childproof cap.

"You cannot do this now. You cannot do this here. You must journey to Aokigahara."

He rolled his eyes at the Yūrei and continued fighting with the lid. "Stupid kid proof caps," he muttered.

"You cannot get the lid off right now. Only when your mind is at a place where you will take the correct dosage will it open. You must go on your journey. You have much to learn."

"I am tired. I don't want to deal with you or anyone. I don't want to go to some creepy forest with dead bodies hanging all over the place. My life has nothing to do with that place."

"Be that as it may, but you still will have to deal with me. You have no choice."

"My life. My choice."

"No. It is not. You must journey to Jukai. You must find your way there. That is all you need to think about – how you will get there. It may be difficult, but you must figure it out. Getting to Japan will be the easy part, but you will find out more when you step on the soil of Japan."

Joshua was getting more frustrated by the minute. He smashed the bottle against his desk. It flew out of his hands and rolled under the couch. He got down on his hands and knees and reached under the couch to retrieve it. He watched it roll further away.

"How do you *do* that?"

"It matters not. Unless you are taking your medication properly, you will not be able to open it. Joshua, you must go to Aokigahara and you must go soon."

"I am not going on any journey. Don't you get it? There's nothing left. I don't even know who I am anymore! Everything I ever believed in was false. I'm not who I was. Nothing will ever be right."

"You will find out who you are. Who you were, who you thought you were matters not. It is who you are that you must discover, and you will learn who you truly are on your journey."

The flames on either side of Minami flickered deep blue for a brief moment.

"I don't care anymore."

He looked up to see there was no longer anything there, just an echo of a voice, "Journey to Aokigahara, Joshua. There is more to this than just you."

He slumped in his desk chair and stared at the picture on his monitor. It wasn't the picture he remembered seeing. He was on a completely different site. The Yahoo news article was about a local man arrested after attacking his wife and stepdaughter. The picture showed a woman and her daughter leaving the local hospital. The daughter was just behind her mother, who was covered in bandages, white bandages in stark contrast to her bloodstained clothing. The girl looked vaguely familiar and was cradling her left arm.

He began to read the article. Halfway through, he realized who the girl was. The one from the gallery. She'd stuck in his mind. Yet, the girl in the picture looked far more fragile now, softer somehow.

Chapter 6

Satisfied with a possible itinerary that would offer her some excitement and feed her need to try new things, Jinn made her flight reservation to Japan for the following week. She really didn't need to worry about the difference in prices between flying out sooner or waiting a week, but despite her having more than enough money, the pre-money part of her still nudged her to wait and save almost a thousand dollars on the flight. She'd also be able to get a first class ticket and, for that long a flight, first class was well worth the extra money.

The remnants of her last trip were still scattered about her apartment. She gathered up some laundry and threw it in the washing machine. She Googled weather in Japan and made some changes to her mental list of what to bring with her. Whatever it was, it needed to fit into her backpack because if it didn't fit, she wouldn't bring it.

Picking up a pile of coats and dirty clothing from near the front door, still lying there from where she'd thrown them when she first got back from Scotland, she noticed a box underneath with a note on it.

Jin-jin,
Saw this outside your door, brought it in when I came to water your

plants. You really need to clean up this disaster! Did the dishes in the sink, was afraid there'd be something ugly crawling around by the time you got back if I didn't. Took your spider plant home with me it needs more TLC than you can give it. Call me! I need to talk to you about Josh.
Susi

Hmmm, Jinn thought. *Never even noticed the damn plant was gone or that she'd done the dishes. Who's Josh?* She shook her head, dropped the armful of laundry and picked up the box. It wasn't too big a box and wasn't heavy at all. She shook it as she walked to the kitchen to grab a knife, but nothing rattled.

Slicing open the tape, Jinn opened the flaps and looked down at an envelope with her name printed on it that was resting on top of crumpled brown paper. She ripped open the envelope and read the letter inside.

```
Dear Jinn,
     The enclosed is the final part of your
inheritance from your grandmother. Aside
from the trust fund, she wanted you to have
these journals. There are five of them span-
ning the last twenty-five years or so. She
requested that you read them all. They are
not all of her journals, but these are the
ones she wanted you to have.
     Sincerely,
     Jonathan M. Reicliff, Esq.
```

Grandmother Alice. The total stranger who appeared out of the mists to leave Jinn more money than some small countries had. Jinn had never even heard of this grandmother until she received a call requesting she come to Reicliff's office several months ago. Her folks were long gone, having died in a car accident when Jinn was just turning eighteen. There wasn't any other family and so she'd just moved on, finding herself an apartment after the bank took back the house for non-payment of the mortgage that she couldn't afford. The house was too big for her anyway and held far too many memories. There hadn't been much life insurance money, just enough to take care of their funerals. Then the money from the newly discovered grandmother arrived. Now this.

Her packing plans forgotten, Jinn removed the brown paper and took out the first of the leather-covered journals. She opened the cover to see that the one she held was from 1989. Wandering into the living room, Jinn plopped into the oversized faux leather chair by the window, and started reading.

May 16th, 1986
Elizabeth is pregnant. I don't know what she is going to do. She says she doesn't want to marry Michael, and that is probably a good thing. I don't like that boy, never did, though Lord knows, I tried. Says she hasn't heard a word from him since she told him that they were having a baby.

Where did I go so wrong with these kids? Justin has turned into a self-serving, holier-than-thou prig and now Liz is having a baby. She says she isn't going to move back home or anything and that she'll be just fine on her own, but I worry so.

The lilacs are blooming on the ridge, the weather is soft and warm and come the beginning of the year, I'll have my seventh grandchild.

"I wonder who Elizabeth and Justin, Jr. are, Jinn mused as she turned the page."

July 27th, 1986
Twins. She's having twins. I know they run in the family, but, dear God. Michael came back and they are attempting to work things out between them. She says he's working, but won't tell me doing what. She just changes the subject.

August 14th, 1986
I saw Elizabeth today. She is showing quite a bit already and has gained weight. She does not have that pregnant glow. She looked tired, miserable and pale. She wasn't happy and really

did not want to talk about the babies at all. There is something she isn't telling me. I tried to talk to her about setting up a nursery and maybe going shopping for cribs or baby clothes, but she just put me off and said she didn't want me spending money. Actually, she said, "wasting" money, but then tried to cover it up.

I fixed her some lunch and some tea, but she barely ate any of it. She wouldn't talk about Michael, plans, or anything. She was just so distant. It just feels so sad when it should be an exciting time.

October 15th, 1986

The doctor says Lizzie will have the babies in January. Michael was gone for close to five weeks but then arrived back like there was nothing wrong. He tossed a bunch of money at Elizabeth and told her to go buy things for the babies, made some comment about how much weight she's gained and left again. That was a week or so ago.

Thanksgiving, 1986

Another holiday and I sit here alone. Elizabeth didn't feel up to traveling. Can't say as I blame her. She didn't want the test to tell her if the twins she was carrying were boys or girls. She wants to wait and be surprised. I wonder if she will make it to January. It is getting very difficult for her to move around. Michael has not been back since October.

Justin and his twins aren't here either. I would love to see them all again, but I haven't seen the grand children since right after Justin Jr and Jason were born. I worry so about Joshua. He is so different from the rest of Justin's brood. Of course, he would be. But I wonder if Justin will ever really accept him. I thought maybe when the twins came along he would, but it just seems as if the poor boy can't measure up. I think maybe Justin marrying Laura was one of the few purely unselfish things he's ever done. And yet, it doesn't ring true. I've never understood why he felt the need to marry a woman pregnant by some other man, and then to treat the poor boy so poorly. Joshua is, truly, the best of the entire brood.

December 18th, 1986

Received a lovely note from Laura explaining about how Justin's work schedule wouldn't permit them to visit again this year and how there simply wasn't a spare inch of space for a guest. She hoped I'd understand. Blah blah, blah.

I finally decided just to send Lizzie some money for Christmas. I expect they'll need it.

Didn't know what to send Justin and Laura for the kids, and when I asked, Laura said not to do anything, that they could provide for the children. They just don't get it.

I should get a cat. They might not mind you, but at least they don't pretend to like you.

Christmas, 1986

I did it. I went to the shelter and got myself a cat! She's a longhaired calico and I've named her Scheherazade. She is just a kitten, beautiful and loves having her coat brushed. She is always purring and has decided her favorite place to sleep during the day is by the front window. At night, she has taken to sleeping on either my feet or my head.

She meows at me and it is almost as if we have conversations. Best thing I've done in a very long time. Should have done this years ago.

Sherry even brought me a present this morning. Didn't know I had mice in this house, but I now have one less mouse. She brought it in and left it on my pillow, and it was the first thing I saw this morning. After I got my breath back, I thought it was funny!

I wonder if I will hear from the children today, or if I should call.

December 31, 1986

Lizzie went into labor this morning and had the twins by early afternoon. I went down to the hospital to see her and the babies. They are both beautiful, all peaches and cream with long, dark, curly hair. They both seem alert and are as alike as two peas. The nurse said they'd be in the hospital for about another two weeks or so, as they are a bit early and need to gain some weight. Michael is back and seems happy to be a dad, but one can never really tell with him.

I hoped maybe I'd see Justin (at least) at the hospital, but Lizzie said he wasn't planning on coming.

January 2, 1987

They still haven't officially named the twins. Lizzie is talking about Emily for the first-born and Emma for the second. Emma isn't doing quite as well as Emily is. She weighs almost a pound less than her sister and is definitely the fussier of the two. I walked with her for about two hours today, but she wouldn't stop crying.

Lizzie says she isn't going to breast feed. I do not agree with her philosophy, but it did mean I was able to feed Emma. She drank almost her entire bottle and fell asleep in my arms.

When I went back to Lizzie's room, she was breast-feeding Emily. Michael told me Lizzie was tired and I should just go home.

Sherry was waiting for me when I got home. She brought me another mouse.

January 5, 1987

I now know why I never seemed to see Lizzie holding Emma. They gave her up for adoption! How could they? She says she just couldn't take care of two babies.

She told me the name of the adoption agency handling Emma, and I filed papers with the courts to adopt her myself. I don't know if that will happen, but I will not lose that child.

February 14, 1987

Today I lost the war, but I did win a battle. I cannot get custody of Emma, but through a bit of finagling I was able to work out an adoption with some friends of mine who have been longing for a child. They will love her and take wonderful care of her. They do not wish me to be an active part of her life, (as they feel it might be confusing down the road) but they will let me know how she is doing.

I will keep my eye on that child, even if it is from afar. They say she is their magical child and will be changing her name to one they feel fits both her and how they got her. She will always be Emma to me.

September 1988

Laura is pregnant. The baby is due in November and she just today got around to telling me. I do not understand them at all. She went on and on about the twins but never said a word about Joshua until I (pointedly I might add) flat out asked. He's fine, was her answer. I don't get it. He's her child. If his real mother is that distant I worry about Joshua.

July 1989

I saw Emily today. She is such a quiet child. Michael has stayed around for the most part and when I saw Emily, she was with her father and they were walking near where they live. She was wearing a bright yellow party dress. At one point, Michael swung Emily high up and onto his shoulders. They were both laughing and she looked happy.

August 1989

Michael was killed in a car accident last week. Just came from Elizabeth's. While Liz was at the funeral, I watched Emily. She keeps asking for daddy.

September 1992
Emma started kindergarten this week. Her hair has lightened to a tawny brown and hangs almost to her waist. It is curly and today she wore a bright red headband to hold it back. She was wearing a plaid smocked dress with a white pinafore over it. She is so beautiful.

October 3, 1992
I saw Emma in the park today. Her mother was standing beneath a large maple tree, looking up at it and yelling. Looking up, I saw Emma, way up in the tree, looking as happy as could be. That girl is quite the tree-climber. She scampered down, and dropped from the lowest branch. I could see her telling her mother about her adventure. Expect she is quite a handful.

December 1992
I got to get both the girls bicycles for Christmas. In fact, that is what all the grandchildren got this year. Emma's was left on their front porch all wrapped up with a large purple bow on it. Both Emma and Emily's bikes were a bright pink, had training wheels and a white basket.

Jinn smiled. She remembered having a bike like that. She'd gotten it for Christmas one year even though her mother had said Santa couldn't afford to give little girls bikes that year. Seems like Emma ended up okay with her adoptive family, after all.

Christmas, 1992
Bought myself a Christmas present too. I love Estée Lauder's Youth Dew perfume and I'd been out for a while. Silly present, maybe, but I do love how it smells. Makes me smile. Sherry sneezes every time I put it on.

Chapter 7

Emily and her mother sat at the dining room table for lunch. Her mother picked at her bowl of soup, pushing the noodles around with her spoon and not eating any of it.

"Mom, you need to eat something. You've hardly eaten a thing since the other day."

"I'm not hungry dear. I'm worried about your father. I don't know if they give them decent food in that place or if he's sleeping all right."

"Decent food? Sleeping all right? Mother, he's in jail. You should be worried about you, about me."

"I am worried, dear. You know, he will be very angry when he gets out. It is all your fault he's in there to begin with."

"*My* fault, Mother? *Oh please!* I am not the one who took a swing at a cop. Nor am I the one who cut you up! *He* did that."

"Only because he was mad at you. You *know* how he feels about this house. He *loves* it. He loves me too. It was just that he was upset."

"Mother, he *abuses* you. Why do you *allow* that? Why do you always cover for him?"

"He does not abuse me. I'm klutzy is all, and I am supposed to do what I can to make him happy. You've never understood that. Wait until you have a man of your own and then you will understand."

"What I *understand,* Mother, is that he wants everything *his* way, he wants my house that Grandma Alice left me and he wants you to be a perfect little doormat!"

"Emily! That is not how it is. He loves you. He just wants you to be responsible. You have a responsibility to us. We raised you. He wants you to reach your potential and not give up on everything you do. It is hard for a man to raise another man's child."

"He knew that way back when. If it was so difficult, maybe he shouldn't have married you! Mom, I hate seeing what he's done to you, what he's doing to you. You need to do what the police say and press charges against him. You need to get the restraining order against him."

"I won't do that. I can't do that. He's your father. He's my husband."

"He's *not* my father, Mother. He's a lousy excuse for a stepfather. Quite frankly, he is *no* father at all. He's not even a real man. He's a slimy excuse for a husband too. Why do you stay with him? I just don't get it."

"Why do I stay with him? I love him. It is my place. And it is your place to give him your respect."

"I can't do that, Mom. He doesn't deserve my respect and he sure as hell hasn't earned it. He's due to get out tomorrow, isn't he?"

"I think so. I'm not sure. The days are blurring together. I don't like the thought of him in there."

Emily stood up suddenly, the force knocking her chair over backwards. "Mother. The man is in jail because he beat you up. He damn near tried to kill you. Don't you get it? He wants me committed just so he can get his paws on this house. He hit me, mom. He hits you. Doesn't that matter?" Emily's voice had risen with each word. Tears streamed down her face. "Doesn't that matter to you at all? Do you think that being in jail for a week will set him straight?

Do you think he won't hit you again?"

"I don't know what to think. I can't think at all with you yelling at me. If you'd just be good and do as he says, there wouldn't be a problem."

"Then I will do what I need to do, Mother. I will file the restraining order to keep him out of this house and away from both of us." Emily grabbed her backpack and stormed out of the house leaving her mother behind, silently crying.

Emily hailed a cab, went first to the bank to retrieve the house documents proving it was hers, and then headed to the court-house. She filled out the necessary paperwork, filed it with the clerk who told her that it would go into effect as soon as her stepfather received the notification at the jail.

Returning home, Emily picked up the dishes still on the dining room table, dumped her mother's soup down the sink and put the dishes in the dishwasher. She poked her head into her mother's room, noticed she was sound asleep on her stepfather's side of the bed, his pillow clutched tightly in arms that were tense even in sleep.

Emily tiptoed in and, taking the throw from the foot of the bed, carefully spread it over her mother. She climbed the stairs to her attic bedroom and slumped in the chair by the window. She hoped the restraining order would keep Nick away from her, her mother and the house, but she didn't have too much faith that it would. *Kind of like a lock,* she mused. *Locks only kept honest people honest. Her stepfather was not honest. Or decent.*

As Emily fell into a troubled sleep, she didn't see the flickering blue flame that burned steadily in the corner of her open window.

Chapter 8

Josh leaned over the rail of the Golden Gate Bridge and looked out at a sailboat skimming along the choppy surface of the water. The wind was brisk and his open jacket fluttered against the reddish-orange grillwork, the zipper making a metallic tapping sound as it blew against it. A seagull landed on the railing a few feet away from him, cocked its head and watched him, one-eyed.

"Don't have any food for you. Not supposed to feed you anyway. Would though, if I had something," Josh murmured. "Unless, you are some weird version of the Yūrei. I wonder if she, it, can do that? Can't believe that I believe in some ghost and I am actually thinking about going to that Aeoki- place. Japan's never been high on my 'to see' list. Actually, it was never on my list at all."

The gull skittered a few feet down the rail, turning so that it was facing Josh head on. It pecked at a piece of loose paint.

"Shouldn't eat that. It's bad for you. Probably contains lead or something." Josh slapped both hands on the railing, causing the gull to take flight. It didn't go far, but landed on the beam-work below him. "Why am I talking to a sea gull? I told you I was nuts!" he yelled to the Yūrei who was nowhere to be seen.

"I actually went and applied for my passport. You hear me? It should arrive any day now and I will go to your Aokigahara. Does that make you happy?"

"You've begun writing again."

Joshua jumped back from the railing as the Yūrei materialized, serenely fluttering about six feet in front of him.

"Yeah, well, yeah, I have. Thinking about keeping a journal of this trip. I can leave it behind me in your suicide forest," he said with a sneer.

"You could," she agreed. "Or you could bring it back with you after your trip."

"Not coming back," he answered firmly.

"You've been painting, too. You don't usually paint people, but you finished that lovely painting of the woman looking out over the sea. Who is she?"

"Don't know," he replied. I think she bought one of my paintings and then I saw her on TV that day you showed up. Of course. You know who she is, don't you? She another of your lost causes?"

"I can't answer that."

"Do you know her name, at least?"

"Yes. She who you have been thinking about is called by several names."

"How helpful."

"It is, actually. I particularly like how you captured her expression. Depending upon the angle, it is almost as if she has more than one, or a viewer could have more than one way of interpreting a single expression.

"You are an excellent artist, Joshua. With paint or words, you portray such nuance and depth. You have captured her essences rather well, I think."

He shrugged.

"Doesn't much matter."

"Ahhh, but it does. You will see. Don't forget to pack a few of your art supplies. You will want them with you. You will need them. *Heiwa no tabi suru*, Joshua."

"What does that mean?"

"Peace be your journey. I wish you a peaceful mind, an open mind. Joshua," she paused, looking troubled. "Joshua, look about you during your travels with the eyes and the insights that you use in your writings, in your artistry. Please." She faded from view, her last words echoing in his mind as twin green flames winked out.

Joshua turned away from the railing and began the walk back to his apartment, thinking he should check his mailbox and see if anything had arrived.

Chapter 9

Jinn read the sporadic entries chronicling the lives of Emma, Emily and Joshua as they grew older. Emily had broken her arm falling off her bike in the spring of '93. Funny, I did too.

"Weird," mused Jinn.

She read that Elizabeth had married again. She learned about Emily's adventures, varying starts, and abrupt stops while trying new things. She read of Justin's death on 9/11 and less and less about Emma. She wondered why.

There were pages and pages about the cat though. Seemed to Jinn that, as the years went by, the cat became her 'grandmother's' world as defined by mouse-presents, purred entanglings of cat and legs and loyalty. There was much written about loyalty, honor and love –or—the lack thereof.

She unfolded herself from the window seat and stood on shaky, cramped legs that had been bent under her for far too long. Getting herself a drink of water, she settled at the kitchen table. There was still one journal yet to go and she figured she might as well plow through the rest.

January 1, 2001
I have some decisions to make and they can be put off no longer. Lives have changed and been

altered by events beyond anyone's choosing.

I still am not certain what to do, but the years are passing and I know my days are numbered as well. The doctor says the aneurism has taken over my aorta from where it comes out of my heart down to where it splits in my groin. I could have five days, five weeks or five months. Then again, I could live for another ten years. He just doesn't know about that. He says, however, that when I go, I will be dead before I hit the floor.

I have put off the contemplation of death for as long as I dare and the time has come to face the inevitable, make my choices and let the devil take the high ground if that is what happens.

January 7, 2004

Do I believe in heaven? I think I do. I want to. but that whole matter of faith makes it difficult to be sure, to be certain. Moreover, as no one has yet come back proclaiming to the world that, "It's really real!" I simply just don't know.

Have I done enough in my life to gain entry to that vaunted place? I believe so. And during this life, I've spent enough time in hell, so I doubt that's an option. Or, when I die, I could just be dead. End of the line. Nothingness. Funny thing is, when it happens, if that is all there is, I won't know, will I?

It concerns me though, the eventuality of a simple ending. One where one moment I am here and the next, absolutely nothing. As if I'd been an ant squashed on a sidewalk or a fly swatted off a screen. End of the road, end of the story. Just a heart that stops beating, a brain no longer capable of thoughts, the ceasing of the me-ness of me, of what and who I am, have been.

What happens to the emotions? To the love that has built up over the years, to the feelings expressed, or not, to the essence of a being?

Do they just stop being too? Is that why we spend our years yearning to be loved, remembered, honored? For nothing other than a few moments of, Remember when mother or grandmother or whoever said such and such? And people hug or make some crass statement or, perhaps, smile a wistful smile. Is all we do in life erased in that fleeting moment when Death grabs us around the throat and does whatever Death does to us? God, I wish I knew.

February 14, 2004

Well, everything is filed appropriately. Possessions delineated to the appropriate (or not!) people. Arrangements all made. If one can see in the hereafter, I shall be beneath that tree on the hill, able to look down to the ocean or up into glorious sunsets.

Or my ashes will, at any rate. Reicliff will scatter them. There will little to no fuss.

Can't trust the others to do it. although Emma or Emily might; they would be the ones, if any.

Lizzie's husband will probably have a stroke. I hope it is terminal. Be the best thing that has happened to both her and Emily in years. I worry so about them, but no one much seems to care what I think. and. thanks to them. I haven't seen Emily in years. Took good care of her though. Iron clad and that bastard won't be able to lay a finger on what is Emily's. Poor, misguided, insecure child. She has so much love in her. but she's like a scared rabbit. Afraid to go after what she wants. So different from Emma. Blame that on that jerk Lizzie married. She's little more than a doorstop these days. or. God-forbid. a punching bag. However, she won't listen or can't hear so why waste my breath. Still, it makes my heart hurt.

Emma's done okay for herself. She has spine that one does. A bit wild, takes too many chances to suit me. Yet she always seems to survive. but then, she's just that: a survivor.

All that is left now are my journals and the letter. I am so glad I had that idea a ways back - to keep my journals separate so that one day the three of them would be able to know what no one will tell them. Yet, they'll know pretty much just their own stories. Maybe it will help them. That and what money I can leave them is the best I can do. I can only hope it is a help to them, that I don't hurt them with the truths they've never known. It was hard coming to grips with the fact that they aren't my truths to tell. Still, once I am gone, there is little anyone can do about it. and I need to know that they will know the truth. I wish I could be there for them then.

March 27, 2004

I wish there was a way the three could meet each other. I doubt that will ever happen. but maybe someday one will stumble across one of the other two and something will click. That thought helps me sleep at night. I need to write the letter. but the right words still haven't come.

September 7, 2004

Emma's parents were killed in a freak car accident. She is truly on her own now. Poor kid, losing her folks twice now. Yet that spine will see her through: that and the money I made sure she got. Reicliff was clever with that. It won't fix losing her parents. but it will help in other ways.

The police said they died instantly. How long is an instant? Was there time to say a last I love you? A final goodbye? Did they even know they were going to die in that instant or were their minds on other things? The usual. the mundane?

I wonder about those things. I think about them all the time. One second you want a cup of tea and the next you are flat on the floor. Oh. God help me—when my time comes. I do not want to die naked in the bathroom. I want to know in that last few seconds, have time for one last look at my world, at Sherry. I want to be able to tell Sherry goodbye.

September 11, 2004

The funeral was today. Is God capricious? Why some in accidents and others to suffer? Why do some linger? When the twin towers fell and Justin died in the rubble, I've always wondered if he went quickly or if he was terrified, if he thought he'd get out or simply knew he had no chance. Or, never knew what hit him.

She looked so lonely and sad at the funeral, but of course, she would. It killed me to act just like another of the many people who came, when all I longed to do was wrap her in my arms. What could it have hurt now? But I gave my word.

Reicliff's after me to write the damn letter. Almost feel as if it will be the last thing I do. Or that when I write it, I will not last that night. I am not ready to die yet. He knows what to do, what to say if I die before it is written.

July 2009

The doctor says the aneurism has grown. Five days, weeks or months. HAH! Got my five years you old reprobate! I bet I'll out-live you!

August 2, 2009

I read in the newspaper today about another person, a young man, who threw himself off the Golden Gate Bridge. So sad. Why, I wonder, would someone do that? I can't imagine life ever being that bad. Debt, illness it goes away or it doesn't, but one simply muddles through. I can't even begin to imagine the state of mind one must be in to do that!

Life is far too short as it is. Is it a giving up? A giving in? An overwhelming sense of hopelessness? One of the ironies of life that some fight to live while others fight to die? Seems like an irrevocable choice: the determination to end one's life. If that effort were put towards living, wouldn't one at least have a chance of surviving and surmounting whatever the difficulties were? I just don't understand! I want to live and I am dying. I don't want to die yet. I have too much to do.

Christmas 2009

I'm glad they let me have Sherry in the nursing home with me. No dead mice this year for Christmas. No family either.

Funny how it isn't going to be the aneurism that gets me. No. Fall on the ice, break a hip, lie in the hospital and catch pneumonia. They tried to take Sherry, but this old woman won that battle. I did.

Lying here in bed, I can either look out the window at a parking lot, or I can look in the oversized mirror on the wall. Sherry sits in the window a lot, and at least she is better to look at than a parking lot full of cars knowing not one of them is here for me. Sad.

Or I can look at the strange old woman lying in the bed, grey hair wound round my head like a turban. They tried to cut it, but I wouldn't let them. My face is a map of wrinkles, a road map, I suppose, of who I am and what I've done in my life. Least the laugh lines equal the worry tracks. Some mornings I wake up not having a clue who that old woman is. I don't feel as old inside as that crone looks! Other days, for a moment's flash I see my mother looking at me. Hmm, I wonder what she'd think?

I'm glad I made arrangements for Sherry. I like to think that maybe one day Emma or Emily will approach Reicliff to find out about her. He knows what to do if one of them should. That gives me some peace.

So lonely. I will give Emma her present now. I will write her letter today, I think. It will be on the last page of this journal.

Jinn's fingers started to turn to the end of the journal, but she hesitated. Little coincidences were beginning to gel in her mind, and she wasn't sure she wanted to read that letter.

Chapter 10

Emily woke to the smell of bacon burning and the sound of screaming from two floors below. Grabbing her robe, she put it on as she ran down the stairs.

"Didn't I tell you to get your daughter to sign the house over to us? It's all her damn fault I spent the last few weeks cooling my heels in jail! Do you know what that's like? She thinks she can keep me out of my home? She's got another think coming, the worthless bitch!"

A sound of a fist hitting flesh and her mother's moan punctuated his previous comment.

Emily entered the kitchen to see her stepfather bending over her mother who lay slumped on the floor. Reaching for the first thing she saw, she grabbed the cast iron frying pan off the stove.

She never felt the hot metal handle searing her hands, nor the grease flying out of the pan as she raised it over her head and brought it down on the back of Nick's head. As he turned, a glazed look on his red and raging face, she swung the pan again.

"You God-damned son of a bitch! Leave my mother alone!"

Years of frustration, fear and anger let loose as the skillet connected again. Yet he didn't go down until he stepped in the bacon grease splattered on the floor. When he fell, his head hit the granite countertop and he went down.

Emily brought the pan down again; fear that he might get up kept her watching him for any sign of movement, until she saw the blood seeping from the back of his head was spreading out over the clean white tiles of the kitchen floor. Dropping the pan, and running to her mother, she noticed the way her mother sprawled on the floor, her neck bent at an impossible angle.

"Mother! Mom, wake up. Mom…" Emily felt for a pulse, but couldn't find one. She slumped to the floor, sobbing as the back door burst open and police filled the room.

Emily sat, her back leaning against the cabinets, her hands, raw with shreds of burned skin blistering in her lap. She was shaking, crying and looking at her hands, the floor—everywhere but at her mother.

One of the cops checked her mother, feeling for the pulse that no longer pulsed.

"I'm sorry, your mother is dead."

"It was all for nothing. He—he hit her and she fell.

Another officer said, "He's dead too."

"I didn't save her," Emily sobbed. She sat there, immobile as the EMT wrapped her hands in gauze, having to lift her to her feet to move her into another room. "I tried to stop him. He wouldn't stop. He wouldn't go down. But it was too late. He killed my mother and I couldn't stop him."

"We need you to come with us," a medical tech said to her. We need to get you to the hospital."

"My mother… I can't leave my mother."

"We are taking care of her. We've got her now."

"A moment please," said one of the officers as he sat on the couch next to Emily. "That is your stepfather in the kitchen, correct? The one you put the restraining order on, right?"

Emily nodded. "It didn't work. He came in anyway. It was supposed to keep him away, but he came in and was yelling and hitting my mother. I didn't think. I had to stop him from hurting her. But it was all for nothing. I couldn't stop him. It was too late." She gulped in a breath of air. "I didn't save my Mom. I can't do anything right. He used to tell me that all the time. I guess he was—he was right."

"He was wrong in every way possible. You did the best you could. You were very brave. You protected her best you could. And he won't be hurting either of you again," the officer soothed.

Emily looked into his kind face and recognized him as the officer she'd seen at the bar.

"But I couldn't save my mother," and she dissolved in tears again.

"Emily, look at me," commanded the officer. "You did your best. You stopped him. He would have come after you next. You did just fine." He looked over to the tech and said, "Take her to the hospital. We have all we need for now."

After he saw Emily led out the front door to the waiting ambulance, he went back to the kitchen, where her mother was being carefully zipped into a body bag. Nick still lay on the floor, his blood pooled beneath his head.

"From the splatter of both grease and blood, you can clearly see the scenario, how she grabbed the pan right off the stove and hit him with it," said the officer who was still documenting the scene. "She had to have been scared out of her wits to hold on to that hot pan. She had hot bacon grease all over her, but she was determined to stop him."

"Good thing she did," commented another officer. "This is the guy we had all the trouble with down at the station. Who'd have thought he'd make bail?"

"Yeah," the photographer continued, "because he would have killed her too. It's clear from the blood on the edge of the counter that he hit that on the way down and, my guess is, the ME will say that was the COD, although she certainly helped him meet his destiny. Given the scene, the documented history, the evidence and her statement, it is pretty clear how this will all go down."

The primary detective on scene huffed out a breath. "I have to write up my report, get the ME's findings and interview the girl again, but from my experience, I'd tend to agree with you. Let's get this garbage bagged up."

Chapter 11

Josh pulled the thick envelope out of the mailbox. *So it was here,* he thought. *My passport. My passport to freedom, to doing what I want without anyone saying I can't!*

He checked the website and made his reservations. He decided to fly into Osaka Airport and then take the train to Aokigahara. Best pricing on flights would have him leaving in just over a week. Perfect! Might as well see something of Japan on his last trip, after all. He spent the next few hours checking out a variety of places he could stop and see. It wasn't until he at last straightened up, rotating his stiffened shoulders, that he realized it was dark and he'd spent three hours finding out about Japan.

Floating serenely behind him the whole time, the flames on either side of her burning with a deep green flame, Minami smiled before winking out of sight.

Chapter 12

Jinn flung the journal across the room. She'd only read a few sentences of the letter from her grandmother? *Adopted? She was freaking adopted? What the fuck? Well, now she knew who the hell Elizabeth was. She was the sleaze who gave her away. What? She was the twin who wasn't good enough? How do you choose between twins?*

She walked over and picked up the journal. She supposed she had to keep reading, but… but adopted…that was just too, too surreal. Maybe there'd be something that would tell her who she really was, because everything she'd always known, assumed, thought was no longer true. She felt as if her reality had shifted.

Who was she? Was this why her eyes were a deep cobalt blue but her parents… her what were they? Why their eyes had both been hazel and they'd been dark haired too. When she'd been little, she'd never thought about it, but as she'd grown older, she began to wonder why she was so different. Mom…yeah…Mom had always said she was exactly how she was supposed to be, but that had never made much sense to her. Sure did now. She bet she looked like that excuse for a baby-factory who'd given her up. Who'd thrown her away.

Tears spilled over now. Swiping the back of her hand against even the thought of crying, Jinn shook her head. *No point to it. Tears never made any difference at all. They hadn't brought back her folks when they'd been in the accident. They hadn't helped growing up when the beautiful ones at school had teased. They wouldn't help now. Damn it. Damn it! Why hadn't her parents ever told her? They were her parents. More than the ones she obviously hadn't been good enough for. Had she been too ... what? Fussy? Wasn't that what her grandmother said she was as a newborn?*

There was a quick double knock at her door and Susi burst in, her arms full of an overflowing grocery bag, three books and a plant.

"Hey, I thought you were back! I've so much to tell you! Wasn't positive you were here, so I thought I'd fix this sty up for you and hey, I got you another plant. Yours is toast. Have you been crying? That dipshit Jeff dump you or something? Good, because you so do not need him in your life!"

When Susi stopped to take a breath, Jinn just looked at her friend and burst into tears.

"What? What? Honey, what happened?" Susie dropped the armful of groceries, plopped the plant on the counter and gathered her friend into her arms.

Jinn just sobbed and handed her friend the journal. "I'm a-a-adopted," she wailed.

"You're what?"

"It's all in here. I'm adopted. No one ever told me. I don't know who I am, anymore."

"Yes, you do. You are my friend, Jinn. The most kickass, badass thrill seeker on the planet! This doesn't change who you are, who you've been. Where you came from, maybe, but not who you are deep down inside. Your folks were awesome. They loved you clear through, you know that! This doesn't change anything."

"But it does. I'm a freaking twin. I have a sister somewhere. There's another me walking around. Oh my god, can you imagine if I'd passed her on the street or if I'd—"

"A twin? Seriously? That is so cool. You have to find her!"

"Wonder if she knows about me? You think she does? The twin tossed out with the trash because Mommy dearest didn't want me? Why didn't she?" Jinn's chin came up. "What's wrong with me? Not a damn, bloody blessed thing!"

"Yeah, she's probably a total bitch," grinned Susi, relieved that the tears were drying up.

"Maybe. At least I'm not," she smiled shakily.

"Well, you have your moments," Susi laughed.

"Yeah, guess maybe I do," Jinn grinned back. "Still, kinda sucks, you know? You go your whole life thinking one thing and them BAM! It is something else completely."

"You'll always be Jinn to me," Susie said loyally and hugged her friend.

"So, how's Josh?" Jinn asked, examining the new plant.

"He's decided he wants to discover himself or something. Oh, and he doesn't want to be a father, or a boyfriend or anything much else for that matter! I moved my stuff outta his place while you were gone."

"Oh, Sus, I'm sorry!"

"Nah, don't be. I'm okay. Just sort of pissed that we wasted so much time together. He'd freak me out sometimes anyway. Go all spiral, spinning into some deep abyss and when he did that ... I could have been a freaking plant for all he ever noticed me. It's all good. Hey, Did ya know there's a package outside your door?"

"What? Huh? No, I didn't. I bet it is the painting I bought from the gallery," Jinn said heading for the door. "It is. Kick ass painting of the bridge. Some dorky guy was just staring at it and I bought it out from under his nose. He looked so sad." Jinn shook her head, laughing as she remembered the look on the guy's face.

She cut the string, pulled the paper from the painting and held it up. "Don't you just love it? Look at the light and the way the art-ist played with the shadows. It is as if it is a bunch of paintings of the bridge, ya know. It's got such dimension."

Susi just stared. "That's one of Josh's. He was working on it when I left. He's been working on that painting for months."

"Really? Wow. Should I say I'm sorry or something?"

"No, no. It's okay. Just took me by surprise. So. Now what? Gonna find your long lost twin?"

"I don't know. I'm headed to Japan in a week or so. There's an aerial stunt show there next month and I've always kinda wanted to go to Japan. They've got some neat places there. Mt. Fuji and some scary sounding forest where people go to hang themselves.

Susi shook her head. "That's crazy tourist shit. No one travels halfway around the globe to see where people die! I know this adoption/twin thing has you spooked but that's just too weird, even for you."

Jinn shrugged. "Sounds different, is all. I need to go do something. I'm not waiting around to see if Jeff ever shows up again, and I can't stand the idea of walking down the street and seeing myself coming the other way. That's just too freakin' weird. Was gonna go anyway, but now I am, for sure. Maybe I'll leave a few days earlier, stop off in Oz. Hell, honestly? If I can get a connecting flight, I'm outta here. Maybe when I get back I'll see if I even want to find my 'long lost twin.' " Jinn shuddered. "Just feels too creepy for words!"

Chapter 13

Emily had been back from the hospital for over week. Her hands were only lightly bandaged now and itched more than they hurt. Neighbors had cleaned up the kitchen and it didn't look like anything at all had happened. The frying pan was still down at the police station, but she didn't care if she ever saw it again. She certainly couldn't even imagine cooking anything in it. She knew she'd never eat bacon again. Even the smell of it in a restaurant made her feel ill.

Everything looked normal, except that it wasn't. It wasn't normal at all when she didn't think and called out to her mother. Then it didn't matter how it looked. The new normal, she thought.

The memorial service, the day after she'd been released, had been rather sparsely attended—the neighbors, a few of her mother's friends, Amy from across the street. They'd made the right noises, patted and pet at her, made inane comments and, of course, brought food which she'd thrown in the trash. There'd been a few reporters there, but she'd just looked blankly at them and turned away. She didn't want to watch them bury her mother's urn, but she couldn't make herself leave. She wouldn't go back there ever again. She hadn't been able to stop her step-father from being buried there after his funeral. It left her feeling hollow, alone and lost.

She sat in the living room, in the dark. It was too much effort to get up and turn on the lamp. She closed her eyes against the pain of re-imagining her mother's last few moments. It didn't matter. It replayed in her head over and over and over again, a record skipping back to the moment she'd first flown into the kitchen. She didn't think she'd ever forget the look on her mother's face, the low, guttural moan, watching her mom slide rag-like to the floor.

She didn't remember much about attacking Nick. She did remember watching a fly buzz around the slowly pooling blood on the bone-white floor. The police had cleared her of any wrongdoing. Closed case, a folder filed. End of story.

"Momma," she whispered in the darkened room. "I tried, Momma. I tried to save you. Why didn't you ever listen to me?"

Tears cascaded silently down her pale cheeks. She sniffled, and pulled the throw blanket up around her shoulders. *It's cold in here. Why is it so cold?*

Sometime in the middle of the night, she woke up from yet another of the dreams that wouldn't let her sleep. Anytime she did sleep anymore, it seemed as if the nightmares haunted her. In some, Nick was back from the dead and chasing her. In others, her mother screamed at her for killing Nick. The one just now had her running in circles, bouncing off of mirrors, but in each mirror was her mother or Nick screaming. Sometimes she saw herself, but she looked different. In the dream even the mirror-Emily was screaming at her. Shaking her head, she wandered back to the couch. Going up to her room, passing her mother's room took just too much energy.

She jerked awake the next morning when she heard a knocking at the front door.

"Go away. I'm not buying anything!" she shouted.

"Got a letter for you here, miss," came a voice from the other side of the door.

"Just leave it on the stoop then."

"I can't miss. You need to sign for it."

Feeling headachy and fuzzy, Emily opened the door. She grabbed the pen, signed her name, took the small box with the envelope on it and slammed the door in the delivery guy's shocked face. Turning, she caught sight of herself in the hallway mirror. Knotted, frizzy brown hair badly in need of a wash and swollen red-rimmed watery blue eyes encircled by shadows. *I look like a roadkill raccoon*, she thought with a grimace. She was still wearing the same clothes she'd worn to the funeral a week ago.

She put the letter down on the table by the front door and wandered upstairs. Taking a better look at herself in the bathroom mirror, she grimaced. *Well, don't I look like the belle from hell?* Letting her clothes land on the floor in a heap, she stripped, turned on the shower to a blistering hot temperature and stepped in. She stood there, just letting the water rain down on her.

Later, when the hot water was all gone and the shower was threatening to turn to ice, she stepped out, went to her room and found some clean clothes to put on. She didn't feel a hundred percent better by any means, but her head was reasonably clear, she wasn't crying and she was beginning to wonder what was in the letter.

Maybe it will sidetrack me for a while, she thought. Going down stairs, she picked up the box, forced herself into the kitchen and made a pot of coffee.

Sitting down at the table, she looked at the return address on the envelope. *Reicliff was Grandmother's attorney*, she mused. Is this something from her?

Opening the letter, she read it silently. *Grandmother sent me journals? I guess that's what's in the box. I wonder why I would have any questions about them.* Emily took her coffee and the thin box upstairs and into her room. She settled down in the chair by her window, putting her mug of coffee on the cherry table. She opened the box to reveal a slim photo album. On the front of it was a short note:

For Emily: because you need to know. Love. Grandma.

Opening the cover, Emily saw that it was a loose-leaf album with plastic sleeves that held, not pictures, but letters. To her.

January 1987
Dear Emily:
I am your grandmother. I will be writing to you from time to time and you will receive these letters when you are all grown up. Right now, you are only a few weeks old. You are a beautiful baby. This is difficult, but I must write this all down so that you, at least some day, will know. You need to know the truth. Some might say that it won't matter, but I disagree. It matters to me. I cannot hope but that it will matter to you and that you will understand why I must do this.

May 1990
Darling Emily:
You are growing so fast, little one. I wonder if you will remember your real father or if his memory will be lost as you are still so young. He wasn't whom I would have chosen for your mother, but when you were born, he really tried to be a good father to you. I disagreed with many things your father did, but I must admit he took very good care of you and loved you dearly. Whatever may be said of him to you over the years, know he did love you.

December 1992
Merry Christmas, darling girl.
I got you a bicycle for Christmas this year. Do you remember getting a pink bicycle with a white basket and a loud jangly bell? I wonder if you will. It didn't take you long to figure out how to ride it. I will always remember you crowing with joy as you rode it down the street.

Spring 1994
Oh, Emily:
I really need to tell you the big truth, but it is so very hard. Do, please, know that I had no choice in the matter: it was not up to me. I hope when you learn all the truth that you will not hate me. I love you so very much, darling girl. Please remember that.

What truth is she talking about? I know Grandma loved me.

What could she possibly tell me that would change that? Emily shifted to a more comfortable position and kept reading her grandmother's spidery script.

September 1996
Emily, darling girl,

You looked so nice this morning as you headed off to school. I watched you from across the street as he was walking with you. You had your new backpack and you were dressed in the sunny yellow "first day of school" dress I bought you.

I love you with long hair and I'm so glad you put your tiny foot down and insisted your mother let you grow it long. You are so pretty, and with those long braids with the yellow yarn ties at the ends, you were a picture this morning.

Spring 2003
Emily,

You are becoming such a young lady. My, the time is speeding quickly by these days. You, so young, probably feel your life stretching out in front of you like a lovely, long scarlet ribbon and that is how it should be.

I wonder sometimes how different your life might have been. Better? While I may think so, who can ever know for certain?

As your ribbon unfurls, mine grows ever shorter. It is as if some days, I can almost feel the spool unraveling and there is little ribbon left. I must tell you soon. Even though I know you will not see these letters until you are grown, until after my ribbon is cut and I go on to the next grand adventure. I just find writing down the words to be so difficult. To find the right way (if there is one) to tell you, to try to explain.

Some days I sit here with the cat, Sherry (who's about a year younger than you are) and wonder if I am doing you a terrible disservice by my silence, but the one hinged upon the other and one choice would have meant others as well. So difficult.

I love you, Emily. Never forget that.

December 2009

Christmas seems like a good time for beginnings and endings. Emily, I am dying. I know I will have been dead a few years or so more when you read this. The attorney will not deliver this to you until after your mother and her husband have passed away. Seems simpler that way, or at

74

least, simpler for you.

Having you read this, as you will be, after the fact that all of us are no longer of this earth, may be taking the coward's way out. You will have to forgive me that, Emily. Honestly, the words have been ready to fall out of me, many times, but it is so difficult to tell you and well, I did promise not to tell, because if I had, then I shouldn't have been allowed to see you ever again. Seeing you grow up, was, and is, very important to me. I don't think I could have stood that. Might that be selfish of me? I expect so, something else you'll have to forgive me for.

It was never my decision that you not know. It was either keep my mouth shut or never see you. End of story.

Family is so very important to me, as, I know it is to you as well. It has to be for you to stick close to your mother no matter what.

I am probably scaring you to death, and I don't mean to. In a way, it may be good news for you. Emily, you have a sister. A twin sister.

I have a what? A sister? A twin? Emily let the journal drop. Her hands were shaking.

"How could I have a sister? Mother, why did you never tell me? How could you *not* tell me?" Emily was yelling to the empty room. Tears spilled and ran unchecked down her cheeks. She shook her head, not so much in denial but because she couldn't process the whole idea. She picked up the journal and started reading again.

I was told her birth name was Emma. I don't know if her adoptive parents changed it or not. Their last name was Lampen. They were very nice people, from what I could see, although very different from your mother and me.

"Emma." Emily tried saying the name. "Emily and Emma." She liked the sound of it. *They sounded like twins,* she thought.

Your parents, your real parents, didn't think that they could afford to take care of both of you. They didn't feel they were equipped to take on two children. I tried, oh, Emily, how I tried to get custody of your sister, but they out maneuvered me and when all was said and done, I was lucky to be able to find out where she went and be able to keep my eyes on her from afar. I wasn't allowed to have any contact with her as her new parents decided against it. They felt it needed to *be a clean break. As long as I never told you and as long as I had no direct contact with her, I was allowed to see and know you. I couldn't take the chance on losing both of you.*

How'd you choose, Mother? How do you pick one child over another? Did you flip a coin? Did I come first or second? Did someone say, "We'll keep the first one or we'll keep the one who is born last?" Was there something wrong with one of us?

"Mother," she wailed. "How could you just give one of us away?"

Emily thought of comments Nick had made over the years. Did her mother regret keeping her over her sister? Did she ever wonder if she'd made the right choice? Did she feel 'stuck' with her and wish she could have traded kids?

I wonder what Emma thought when she found out, or does she not know about me yet? Emily wondered about that, and kept on reading.

Her adoptive parents died a few years ago and I have lost track of where she is, but my attorney has assured me he will find her, so that she will know about you as well.

I am reasonably sure that she is still in the Bay-area, but I am not sure.

You are identical twins. She is bright, sassy, and energetic. She strikes me though, as something of a lost soul. You are much the same in that respect. Yet, you are also like two sides of a coin, for where you are less likely to jump; she will fly in feet first. Where you are tentative, she is confident. You are both beautiful young women.

"Is that a nice way of saying I'm the boring one, Grandma?" Emily whispered. "Did I let you down too? Do you wish it had been her you could talk to and see? Two sides of a whole sounds like I got only half of the me I *should* have been, and she got all the rest. Maybe I'd have been different if instead of two of us, there had been only one." Emily sighed.

With no close family any longer, the time has come for you to know the truth. My wish is for you both to find each other. You need each other.

Dear, dear Emily. I hope you can forgive this old woman her secrets. Find your sister. In doing so, I suspect you will each find yourselves.
 Know I have and always will, love you both.
 Grandma Alice.

Emily hugged the journal closely, wrapping her arms around herself. *Oh Grandma, of course I forgive you. You had no choice.* Her mother was a different story. *Mother, how could you?*

She walked over to her window. The evening breeze wafted in, someone, somewhere had a fire going in their back yard. Faint laughter rippled on the breeze. *At least someone is having a good night tonight with friends or family. Have we ever had a fire outside? No. I bet Emma's family did. Why did I have to get stuck with Nick? I bet she had a nice family, a good one where no one got hit, abused, or yelled at.*

"Why wasn't I good enough? Why did I have to be the one you kept? Now I have no one!" Emily was yelling at the ceiling as if she could see through to heaven or wherever her mother now was. "She probably hates me for being the one given away."

Crying now, Emily threw herself on her bed. *Feel like I can't do anything right. Sure didn't here. Only family I have now is a twin who will hate me too.*

Her hands, throbbing again from the not yet healed burns, had her reaching for her prescription.

Thirty some pills. I could just go to sleep and I wouldn't dream…

Even though the bottle didn't have a childproof lid, she couldn't get the cap off.

"You cannot do this now. You cannot do this here."

"Whaaa— who?" Emily looked around, fear widening her eyes. There was no one here. *Must have imagined it,* she thought.

"No, you didn't imagine anything." Floating near her window, Emily could see a white figure, well half of one. There were bluish green flames on either side of her head.

"Whaa—? Who are you?"

"That doesn't matter. What does matter is that you cannot do what you are thinking about doing. Not here. Not now. You must journey to Aokigahara, Emily. Only on your journey will you find the answers you seek, and more, the answers to the questions you don't want to ask."

"What's Aokigahara? Is it a place?"

"It is a forest in Japan. You need to go there." The faint image flickered.

"But why?"

"Because you must. Don't question the whys for which you have no answers. Go to Jukai, to the forest Aokigahara, Emily. It is the journey you need to take. Find the answers to the whys which will make a difference." With these words, the white mist vanished leaving the twin flames to go out a second later. Emily swiped the back of her hand across her eyes, rubbing the tears away.

"Aokigahara." She said the word aloud, liking the way it sounded. She stood up and opened her laptop. *Might as well check it out, it isn't like I have anything better to do…*

PART *Two* : THE JOURNEY

Chapter 14

Josh added the final touches to the painting of the girl he'd been working on. She sat on a window seat looking out at the bridge in the distance. She looked sad in the light of a candle that flickered nearby. He'd been working on it on and off since he'd seen the girl on the news after she bought one of his pictures at the gallery. Both times he'd seen her, she had looked sad, lost and lonely. There was just something about her that had crept into his mind and stayed there. Something about that look in her eyes, the stubborn angle of her chin, the determined mouth that didn't quite want to smile, but refused to settle into a frown. He didn't know why she was stuck in his mind, but she didn't seem to want to go away, and when that happened, he simply knew he needed to paint it out. Usually, it worked, but thus far, it hadn't this time.

He'd been back to the gallery, but he hadn't seen her again. He rinsed out his brush and set it neatly with the rest of his brushes. For all he knew, it was the last painting he'd ever paint. *It was a good one to end on*, he thought. *Maybe even the best one he'd ever painted and he almost never painted people. People didn't interest him, as a rule. They wore too many masks.*

Grabbing his phone off the coffee table, he took a picture of his painting. It wasn't something he usually did; normally once the painting hit the canvas and left his mind, he was done with it, but this one was different. He felt as if he'd allowed some of his own essence into it, as if his blood was mixed in with the oils that became the woman he'd painted. He'd bring the painting to the gallery in the morning; they'd worry about framing it. He should have enough time before heading to the airport. He'd paid the extra to book a direct flight into Osaka and then would rent a car to drive north. He'd sleep on the plane. *Funny,* he mused, *between the painting and actually getting excited about the trip, he hadn't felt quite so much out of control. His mind wasn't spiraling quite as much.* He grinned; *it was all the means to an end, wasn't it?*

Josh finished packing, being sure to put his journal in with the clothes he'd chosen. One backpack held everything he'd need. He'd thought about bringing at least some brushes with him, but after painting 'Lost Girl' as he thought of his recent painting, he really didn't feel the need or pull he usually did and so left them on the table next to his easel.

Looking around his small apartment, he realized there was nothing much of any real value he was leaving behind. Not the journals. He'd read them over several times now, but all they did was raise questions that he couldn't answer, making him feel out of place as if he were a step aside from where he actually was, like the second image in a vibration he couldn't quite control.

It was that control thing that would get his mind racing, spiraling, wobbling and drove him crazy. No need for the journals. He didn't want them or anything they represented.

He smiled as he looked at his music, his books, and his assorted knick-knacked memories of trips or events. Memory served well and they were just things after all. Even his beloved 'painting book' seemed as if it had served its purpose. His rent was paid through the end of the next month, so it would be a while before anyone would even figure out he was gone. If they did.

No, there was nothing left for him here, nothing that

mattered at all. He flopped down on his bed, and, for a change, drifted quickly and peacefully off to sleep.

Chapter 15

Emily spent the rest of the night looking up and then finding out about the Forest of Sorrows, the second most common place in the world where people went to commit suicide. Number One, she found out, was right there in San Francisco, at the Golden Gate Bridge. *Why,* she wondered, *was she being sent to the second most common place? Was it because she was doomed to second place finishes, or simply never finished anything? It fit. She wasn't even an original, being a twin, she was a second edition. Even she had to admit that.*

Clicking from link to link, she watched a movie a director had filmed that captured and followed up on every suicide off the bridge in an entire year. It was horrifying to watch and yet, she could not tear herself away from watching body after body falling, grasping at air as each tumbled inexorably into the cold waters of the Bay. She read of a young man who changed his mind a split second after letting go and managed to survive.

In an interview, she read how harbor seals, 'white wraiths' someone had called them, would circle around and around some of the jumpers, keeping their heads above water until they could be rescued.

Emily thought about the pictures she'd seen of harbor seals. When they were sitting on their haunches, with their flippers hanging down, they *did* sort of look like her white wraith.

Survivors were split fifty-fifty between those who tried again and those who got help or were able to modify medications to keep themselves on an even keel. *They are different from me,* she thought. *I'm not chronically depressed or think everything is hopeless. I simply don't see the point. Why go on when there is nothing to go on for? I can't seem to do anything right, I couldn't save my mother. I bet my twin would have.*

She gasped. She could have sworn she felt as if someone had thrown a bucket of icy cold water at her.

"You need to stop feeling sorry for yourself!" The Yūrei was back. At least she knew what it was now, and, boy, did it ever look angry.

"You have no clue how much better off you are than so many helpless, hopeless souls out there. You should be ashamed! Your barriers are gone now. There is *nothing* holding you back from anything—except the barriers you give yourself!"

"You don't know anything about me," Emily said, angry now herself. "You don't know what it is like to have half your soul ripped away. To know there is a part of you somewhere who is like the face in the mirror."

"You'd be surprised what I know and yes, what I have felt. You talk of being a twin. I, too, am a twin. I know what it is like to have feelings entwined so strongly for another that it goes beyond mere love. I know what it is like to have someone reach in with grasping fingers and yank your very heart, still bleeding, from your chest and throw it away. To have this done to you because you have what they have not and what they want more than life itself. I know 'hopeless.' I know utter, total death of feeling. I know what it is to lose love and family, trust and heart." The Yūrei's voice, which had been shill in her anger quieted.

"I know what it is to have that very other half be the one to tear it all away because she could never have gained all I had for herself. And I know, truly know, what it means to be stuck here, half in this world, half in the next and know that the man for whom she did this, the man she took away, never, until the day he died, ever, had even an inkling that it was she he was with and not me.

"You," and the Yūrei's voice grew stronger, "you have a chance, moreover a choice to find her, find yourself and find all you have sought, but you will not find it here. You will not find it this moment. You must go to Aokigahara, Emily. There is much you need to do; there is much you need to learn. You will not do that here in this safe, little room at the top of the house. Go to Jukai, Emily. Go tomorrow. For you. For her." She paused, "For me." With those words, the Yūrei's flames sparked brightly blue, then both the flames and her voice faded and she was gone.

Chapter 16

The airport was busy for the middle of the day. It was long past the morning rush, but lines snaked around, writhing in impatience, as bags were checked and tickets handed out. It had been pouring all morning, and the smell of wet hair and clothing reminded Jinn of wandering the streets of New Delhi during the monsoon. She wrinkled her nose. She cut across three lines in an effort to reach one line that seemed to be moving faster than the others were. In front of her, a family of five waited. The three young children wriggled, yelled, climbed on their bags, and fought over a teddy bear while the parents jointly raised exasperated eyes to the heavens above as if seeking help or some godly finger to poke down and quiet their offspring.

God, I hope they give them something to knock them out on the plane! Maybe they will be on a different flight. She could feel a headache beginning to pound behind her eyes. Nothing was going the way she'd planned. Her flight to Sydney had been over-booked, so she'd decided just to go straight to Osaka. *It was a long freakin' flight, especially since she'd be stuck in coach for twelve hours.* She grinned. *At least she'd be getting there before she left! Gotta love crossing the dateline!*

She scanned the time board and then, as she moved forward a few steps, looked around the chaos that was the San Francisco Airport. Running her fingers through her damp hair, she was startled when she ran out of hair. Grinning at herself she remembered hacking the length of it off last night. Now it was choppy and short and she wondered once again why she hadn't done this years ago.

She saw a man with a backpack just like hers three lines over and thought he looked vaguely like the guy from the gallery, but then the line moved forward again and it was her turn. She watched the family, now hand in hand, head for the boarding area and overheard the mother say she hoped the weather was fine in Sydney. *Oh, thank God! A different flight.*

"Yes," she said, handing her ticket and passport to the agent, "My name is Jinn Lampon. I have an open flight to Osaka."

Josh had been in line for some twenty minutes and was almost to the front of the line when he saw her go through the pass-way to airport security. He wanted to rush over there, but it would have done him no good, as he didn't have his boarding pass yet. He wondered where she was headed and if, just maybe, he'd see her in one of the boarding areas. *Not,* he thought, *that I've got a clue exactly what I'd even say to her. He could hear himself saying, 'I painted a picture of you.' How lame would that be?*

He handed his ticket to the pretty dark-haired agent and smiled.

"Oh, first class, sir. You needn't have waited in this line. Here is your boarding pass and seat assignment. Please go through those doors on the right for security."

"I don't go through over there?" he said pointing towards where the girl had just gone.

"No sir. That is security for all the coach passengers. Next!"

He grabbed his backpack and headed reluctantly to the right. Just before he entered, his eye caught a flash of bright yellow, as if the sun itself had invaded the dreary airport. *It looked just like… but wait, she'd just gone through security. It couldn't be.* People jostled behind him and he walked into the first class lounge, thinking he was going nuts and seeing her everywhere.

⌁ ⌁

Emily shrugged her shoulder, easing the weight of her duffle bag she'd slung over her back. Wearing jeans and a bright yellow denim jacket, she smiled at the children playing quietly in front of her. She wondered where they were going.

"Hi! We're going to our Grandma's house. It's a long way! We get to go on an airplane. You going on an airplane too?" asked a little girl with long hair tied up in pigtails, a doll in her arm and a bright smile.

"Yes, I am," answered Emily. I'm going to Japan."

"Is that farther away than Michigan?"

"Well," Emily answered, "they are both pretty far away from California. I hope you have a nice visit."

"We will. Our Grandma's the greatest!"

"Come children," interrupted her mother, "it's time to go to the plane."

"Bye," chorused the two children before following their mother.

"I have a flight to Osaka, Japan. Here are my ticket and my passport," Emily said to the ticket agent.

"Are you going on vacation?" asked the bubbly raven-haired woman.

"Sort of, I guess. I'm doing, ah, research."

"Beautiful place for it," commented the agent, handing her a boarding pass and telling her to head off to her left. "Your flight leaves in an hour and a half. Too bad you didn't have tickets on the

1:00 p.m. flight; you'd just about have time to make it to the gate. But your flight isn't nearly as full, so you may well have room to stretch out!"

Emily went through security and found a place to get something to eat while she waited in her boarding area. Was she crazy? *Here I am flying to Japan because I had some sort of crazy imagination hiccup. Seemed real,* she mused, *but it couldn't possibly have been. Could it? No matter,* she told herself, *it's better than worrying about a long lost twin who probably hates me.*

Chapter 17

Josh didn't have anyone sitting next to him, so he stretched out, taking up both the first class seats. He shifted yet again, but he couldn't seem to get comfortable. He couldn't get the girl out of his mind. That, and the fact that he thought he'd seen her twice inside of ten minutes. *Impossible.*

He took out his phone and looked at the picture he'd taken of his painting. *What was it about her,* he wondered, *that kept her circling around the edges of his mind?* Here he was heading to Aokigahara, and now he finds a woman who caught at his heart the way Susi never had, never could. *I don't even know the first thing about her! I wonder where she is going.*

Curled as he was, facing the back of the seat, he shoved the ridiculously small pillow into a more comfortable position. "You'd think," he muttered softly, "that the pillows in first class would be bigger than this." He punched it again.

A faint flicker caught his eye. "Joshua, I am glad you are going on your journey. You will find answers to many of your questions along the way, even as you realize that the answers will only bring more questions. Find the answers, Josh.

"One more thing. I am glad you are painting again, as your creations are a part of your answer." With that, the Yūrei flared brightly and then flickered out in a soft, blue flash.

Back in the third to last row of coach, Emily toed off her shoes and stretched out; enjoying the fact that she at least had three seats to herself. She'd balled up her jacket under her pillow and still, wasn't comfortable. The lumps from the seat belts poked at her hip. She'd tried reading the new Mara McBain book she'd found in the book kiosk at the airport, but as good as the story was, her mind had wandered. She thought about the previous night and her strange visitor. *Only I'd have a ghost, if that's what the Yūrei is, yell at me,* she thought.

She'd spent most of the night on her computer surfing various sites offering information about Jukai. She couldn't imagine hanging herself, as most of those who went into the forest did. She had just wanted to sleep her way into forever where there weren't missing twins or abusive stepfathers. She just wanted peace, where she wasn't trying to take care of her mother. It was too much to think about, to worry over—and now the whole sister thing... .

She'd sent an email to the attorney saying she was headed out of town on an extended trip, but that when she returned (and she hadn't said just when that would be) she'd think about having him find Emma. She couldn't think about it now. For that matter, she wouldn't think about her at all. She really had nothing to do with her anyway, did she? It didn't matter. Nothing much mattered anymore. Emily closed her eyes and fell into an uncomfortable and restless sleep. She didn't see the Yūrei flickering softly overhead nor did she hear her whisper, *"Heiwa no tabi suru"* before winking out of sight.

Jinn sat scrunched in her window seat looking out over the endless ocean that was quickly vanishing as night raced to overtake them. Changing her flight at the last minute meant that the money she would have spent on a first class seat now barely covered a seat in coach, but she hadn't wanted to blow any more for it and was too excited about the idea of Japan to change her plans even further. The agent had offered her a seat on the following flight out, one that wasn't nearly as full, but she hadn't wanted to sit around the airport for another two hours when she was already going to be spending twelve hours on the plane. She scrunched and shifted in her seat, deciding she could put up with anything for twelve hours. They'd flown over Hawaii several hours ago, but she'd been on the wrong side of the airplane to see it when the pilot announced they were flying past it.

She'd spent an hour or two talking to the passenger across the aisle. They shared an interest in extreme sports and realized they been at several events at the same time. He was heading to the Japan Paragliding competition in a few weeks. They both were going to the International Parachuting competition.

They talked chute talk for a while, places where they'd both done paragliding and they shared favorite beaches for surfing. Although he'd told her that he was twenty-five, he began to remind her too much of Jeff. So, she'd shut him down saying she needed to sleep.

What she'd wanted to do was think. Think about her sister, her twin. Who, honestly, had a twin she didn't even know about? Really? *It could be cool;* she mused, but then wondered once again about why *she* was given away. She bet that the one they'd kept must have had it good, never worrying about a blessed thing. *My life's been good. Maybe even better than yours, sis,* she thought to herself. She supposed she should try to find her when she got back, better than tripping over her at a gallery or while crossing the street. *Maybe.*

What was she like? Maybe she was married to some

rich guy and had three kids. Maybe she was a drug addict. Who knew? Didn't twins separated at birth usually turn out pretty much the same? Jinn remembered reading an article about twins once. Living clear across the country and yet they'd married guys with the same name, had similar jobs and named their kids the same names. *I'd just die if she was married and had a kid named Jinn! Does she like cats? Can she sing? I wonder if she surfs.* Jinn shook her head. *I shouldn't go there. We probably won't even like each other. I still wonder why I was the one adopted. Tossed out, like an unwanted Christmas gift. 'Here, I already have one of these.'*

Jinn shuddered, wriggled around in her seat and closed her eyes. *When I get back. I won't think about her 'til I get back.*

Chapter 18

In the way that dreams don't always make sense, Joshua was dreaming he was watching a play about Aokigahara. He was sitting on an overstuffed and scratchy chair in the front row of a cavernous theater. There was a smell, damp and musty, of decaying leaves. Heavy velvet curtains, deeply magenta, were drawn across the stage and, in the orchestra pit, he could hear flutes and violins playing. Around and behind him, the audience was full of hundreds of Yūreis. They writhed and flickered— blues and greens, their half bodies floating above each seat. Next to him serenely floated his Yūrei, Minami.

"It's only a play, Joshua. You've bought your ticket, now you must watch as it all plays out."

The curtains slowly, slowly creaked open. Joshua could hear the sound of the ropes moving through pulleys, of the one pulling the ropes grunting, as if it took extreme effort or the ropes were incredibly heavy.

It was all dark on stage. Light rose fractionally. Up center, covering the entire rear of the stage was a screen, but as yet, the light barely lit the top of it, leaving the rest of the stage in darkness. As the light brightened, it revealed what he first thought was a black and white photo of Mt. Fuji. It was the same one everyone saw on travel posters or calendars. Glowing now, beyond the darkened silhouettes of trees on stage, was a sunrise, which grew in size as colors blossomed. Then, he realized it wasn't a picture, but a movie showing the sunrise catching the snow-covered peak. Soft clouds around the summit were shades of pale pink until, as the sun rose higher, it turned the snow on the mountain blood red. The music changed now, with the addition of bassoons and a cello.

As the light on stage rose, the haunting music grew louder and he could see first the twisted, grotesquely misshapen trees. Then he could see bodies twisting and turning in some spectral dance, but they weren't hanging from ropes twisted around their necks. Instead, they were each hanging limply by a wrist, some by their right wrists and others, by their left. Some wore ragged remnants of clothing, signifying that they'd been there a long while. Others wore clothing that showed they'd only been there a short time.

Spotlighted stage right, he saw himself dangling by his left wrist, dead. His face was blue, but where his eyes should have been, two small round mirrors reflected the audience. He could see himself reflected in those twin mirrors. His art supplies and his journal were lying on the ground in front of him. All around him his paintings were leaning at odd angles, propped up against the trees or displayed in broken frames in the branches.

The audience-Josh wondered if there was some special significance to the people hanging by their left wrists. The dream seemed to pause as he thought, *Manus Hand, manifestation.* Art. He looked over to the Yūrei. She barely smiled and shrugged.

"It could be that dreams involving the binding of a wrist have to do with someone giving up or feeling that others control their lives," said the Yūrei in the seat on the other side of Josh.

"Like feeling that my hands are tied," Josh mused.

"A loss of productivity," continued the same Yūrei.

The Yūrei behind him added, "the left hand in many cultures is the bad hand or the unclean hand. This could be further interpreted to mean that one needs to wash it, or wash away negatives."

"Also," added another from a few rows back, "if you dream that your wrists are injured, then it implies that you are not reaching out to others enough. Alternatively, the dream suggests that you are taking more than you give."

"Please," interjected Minami, "let the dream unfold. It is up to Joshua to learn what he may from the dream."

There was movement stage left on the barely lit scene. In the shadows, he saw a girl fall. Her right wrist tangled in knotted rope. She was struggling and choking in her death throes. He couldn't see her clearly, for it was still too dark.

The music changed, became harsher and more hopeless-sounding, bringing in tympani drums to offset the gentle flutes. As the light grew slowly brighter, trombones blared a chord change to e-major. *Not unlike,* he thought, *the discordant final screech in Bolero.* The light suddenly went to a garish brightness. The girl, no longer struggling, hung silently. She was wearing a dingy, yellow jacket.

He awakened with a jolt. It was still dark on the plane and he could hear the sounds of a man softly snoring a few seats away and the lady behind him coughing. He shivered. The dream had felt so *real.* Why was she there? Why was she hanging in Aokigahara? Images swirled in his mind and he reached for his journal. He couldn't paint what was in his heart, so he would write what was in his mind instead.

Chapter 19

Attention all passengers, this is your Captain speaking. Due to inclement weather at our destination, this flight is being rerouted to Nagasaki. We will endeavor to get you to your final destination as soon as possible once it is safe to fly into Osaka. The airline will issue travel vouchers for the later flights. For those not wishing to continue on in their flight, there are rental cars, buses and trains to facilitate getting you to your destination. The airline will offer payment vouchers for either train or bus service. We sincerely apologize for any inconvenience, but it is with your safety in mind that we will be landing in Nagasaki in twenty minutes.

Swell, thought Joshua. *Guess I'll be renting a car after all.* He grimaced as he took his first life-saving sip of coffee. It didn't taste like coffee at home, and he wondered what brand it was. It was hot and strong, however, so he drank it down as he thought about getting maps and driving north. Then he wondered if he even could rent a car here. Did he need an international driving license? And, which side of the road did they drive on in Japan?

Back in coach, Emily stretched and considered her options. She really didn't want to wait around for another flight. She supposed she could get a train or a bus. No way was she up to driving on the other side of the road.

The plane landed and passengers slowly gathered their belongings and trudged off towards the baggage area. Since she just had her carry-on, she bypassed most of the crowd and headed for customs. She passed through without incident and then paused, looking about as she tried to figure out where to go. *Train or Bus?* She wandered over to where various schedules were posted. *Good thing they are in both English and Japanese,* she thought, *otherwise I'd really be in a mess!*

Emily looked at the various train schedules and decided to check out the bus routes. It might take longer by bus, but then she really wasn't in a hurry. She thought about how she'd see more of the country and the small towns and villages. There wasn't a bus leaving that would get her to Osaka for another couple of hours, so she decided to find a place to get something to eat. Outside the airport, and across the street, she saw a variety of vendors. *I'd better change some money.*

Josh checked out the rental cars and found that the passengers on the three previously rerouted flights had wiped out any available rentals. He thought about taking the train for a moment, but decided to take the bus. "See more of the local stuff," he said softly.

Changing his money at a nearby kiosk, he saw something out of the corner of his eye that almost had him forgetting to grab his money.

Was she really here too? Had she actually been on his flight? Maybe back in coach? He started after her, but she was lost in the crowd. He headed outside and saw her across the street at one of the food vendors. *She was here!*

He started to cross the street and then stopped. *What do I say to her?* "*Yeah, well, I saw you in SanFran and I painted your picture and I've been obsessing about you for a month or so?*" *Yeah, that'd fly. Like a rock.*

He watched her buy some food from the vendor and wandered closer. He heard her say, "Thank you," and found his opening.

"Hi, you from the states too?"

"I, um, yeah. I just flew in from San Francisco. I was supposed to be flying to Osaka, but my plane was diverted here. Weather or something."

"Me too. I mean my plane and San Francisco too, actually. I'm Joshua," he said holding out his hand to shake.

"I'm Emily," she smiled back. "So, you taking the train north?"

"Actually, I'm thinking more along the lines of the bus. I was going to rent a car, but they're out of them. I guess quite a few planes were rerouted due to the weather. There's a train in about thirty minutes and then again tomorrow, or an hour's wait or so for the bus. I figure I'll see more by bus and I'm not really on a deadline or anything, so ..."

"Me neither. Where are you headed?"

"Um, Mt Fuji, eventually. I've always wanted to see it."

"Me too. I kind of want to see the real Japan, you know? Not the big touristy places, but the real places where people live and work. I'm thinking I want to see the little towns, the villages, maybe a shrine or two."

"Taking the bus will pretty much guarantee that, I think. There aren't any direct ones. From here the bus goes through Nagasaki to Hiroshima to Osaka and then on to Tokyo on — quite a roundabout sort of route. It will take a few days, I expect."

"After that long flight, I just want to get on my way and then find some place to stay each night." Emily patted her camera. "I'm hoping to take lots of pictures."

"I figure after a couple of hours, if I see someplace, I'm going to stop too. I want a shower and a bed that doesn't have seat belt sabers stabbing me!"

She giggled, and he thought what a nice sound it was. They'd wandered over to where the bus stop was and settled onto a bench, only to see a lumbering old rusty bus belch its way to a stop.

"Is that the bus?" she asked. "It isn't due for a while yet."

"Bus come when it come. Schedule only for paper. You take bus now?" A small woman, beautifully dressed in eastern clothing, pointed at the bus.

Emily smiled at the woman and looked at Joshua. It wasn't what she was expecting at all.

"I guess if we want a seat we'd better grab one while the grabbing exists. Don't seem to be too many seats." Josh looked at her hopefully. " C'mon. It'll be an adventure."

She hesitated for a moment, and then shrugged. "Why not."

She paid her fare and climbed into the bus. The seats were old vinyl and were cracked, letting the horsehair stuffing show through. There was no glass in the windows. As she and Joshua settled next to each other on the tiny double seat, she watched as more people scrambled on board. Then the bus lurched forward, and they were on their way.

Three hours later, the bus creaked into a small town, but it was one that had a motel across the street from where the bus came to a halt. Emily nudged Joshua, who was sound asleep.

"Wake up. There's a hotel here. I'm done for the day. According to the schedule, there's another bus in the morning. I wanted to say goodbye."

"Will you think I'm strange or something if I get off too?. I need to walk for a bit and, after I see if I can get a room, I want to just wander around."

"No, I don't think you are strange," she said shyly. "I just want to go to sleep."

They climbed off the bus and they both were able to get rooms. Saying she'd see him in the morning, Emily let her clothes fall to the floor, took a fast shower and crawled into bed.

Josh dumped his bag in his room and went out to explore the town. There wasn't much to it, but it was pretty in a gently impoverished way. People nodded and smiled at him as he walked. He stopped and watched some local children playing soccer in a rutted field next to a restaurant. Taking a seat at one of the tables on a porch, he merely pointed at an item on the menu, having no clue what he was ordering.

It turned out to be rice and chicken and a couple of other things about which he had no clue as to their identity. But it tasted good. As he ate, he thought about Emily. She didn't seem as sad as the last time he had seen her. He wanted to tell her that he'd seen her before, but he wasn't sure how to bring it up, let alone the reason why he'd come to Japan. Comfortably full, he walked back to the hotel, went to his room and passed out.

Jinn's plane also had been diverted. Complaining about inconvenience and lousy weather, she'd pushed and shoved her way off the plane and headed towards the car rentals. As a line quickly formed behind her, she was glad she'd hurried and beat the rush through customs. She was able to rent a small car, filled out all the forms, signed her life away on the numerous dotted lines, showed her international driver's license, grabbed a map and headed out the door. Behind her, the long line held people doomed to disappointment, but she was on her way north.

She went to the pick-up point and found she'd rented a shiny, iridescent blue sedan. She got in, familiarized herself with the controls, plugged in her iPhone, turned the key and, with music blasting from the car radio, turned out onto the road. She followed the map, sticking to highways for about three hours and then pulled off at an exit where she could see hotel signs flashing.

She rented what was probably the smallest hotel room she'd ever seen, took a shower down the hall and returned to her room in her bathrobe, only to discover that this hotel had never heard of room service. Getting dressed again and running her fingers through still damp hair; she headed out to find food. Back in her room an hour later, she curled up on her bed thinking the airplane seats had been more comfortable than this and finally, finally fell asleep.

Chapter 20

Emily was running through a waist-deep lake of blood watching ducks swim by quacking in Japanese. They all seemed to be quacking at her, trying to tell her something, but she couldn't understand them. Behind her, she could hear Nick shouting her name. Looking over her shoulder, she could see him catching up to her. She tried to move faster, but the ducks kept getting in her way. As a hand grabbed her shoulder, she woke up, shaking in the middle of her room.

Her whole body ached and her eyes felt as though they were full of sand. She saw that it was getting light outside, checked her phone and saw that it was early morning. Looking out her window, she saw the sky etched in pale pink wisps of clouds. She stood at the window and watched the wisps turn into bright red ribbons but then slowly faded as the sun rose higher in the sky. She dressed, repacked her bag and headed out to find somewhere to eat. She saw Joshua sitting at a small restaurant down the street and walked over. He smiled in welcome and asked her to join him.

"Want a bite of this to see if you like it? I have no clue what it is, but it's really good. Did you sleep well? I slept like the dead. The bus is supposed to be here in about an hour. Give or take," he added remembering the day before.

"This is delicious!" When the waitress came around, she ordered the same thing Josh had and settled for tea, as coffee was not on the menu.

Answering his earlier question, she replied, "No, I really didn't sleep all that well. I woke out of a horrid nightmare. Must be the traveling and all," she added sheepishly.

"It happens. You are okay now, though, right?"

"Yes." Her food arrived and she realized just how hungry she was. "I never ate anything last night."

"I ate here. I wandered around town and watched some kids playing soccer. It was nice. I was looking at the map earlier. It looks like we will be driving through some mountainous areas today. It should be pretty and give you some chances for taking pictures."

She smiled. "That will be great. I hope I have enough time to get some photos before we leave today too."

After they finished eating, they meandered around the village while Emily took picture after picture. Josh liked the way she would focus in on a small red flower growing out of a rock wall or on a snowy white bird perched atop a roof. They were about a block away from the bus stop when he noticed that what he thought might be the bus had arrived. Laughing together, they ran to catch it.

The bus was very different from the one the day before, and it was even older. This ancient VW bus had to be at least forty years old. There was no glass in the side windows and the seats were wooden benches. People climbed aboard carrying chickens, children and baskets of food.

"Well, this certainly will be an adventure," Emily commented as she took a picture of Joshua squeezed next to an old man carrying two scrawny chickens and a fat red rooster. On the other side of Emily was a woman with an infant. Instead of holding the baby in her arms, the woman had tied it against herself with a bright yellow cloth wrapped around her own waist and chest. The baby almost looked like a papoose, except that it was up against her mother's stomach instead of on her back. The wide band of yellow supported the baby's head and then continued over the woman's shoulder and fastened under her arm.

As the bus bounced and rattled along, clearly having no shocks, they traveled up a narrow and bumpy mountain road. Emily turned this way and then another, taking pictures. At the next stop, enough people got off the bus to allow Josh and Emily now to sit together. Joshua motioned for Emily to take the inside seat by the window.

"Emily," Josh began a few miles up the road, "I need to tell you something. Please do not think I'm a stalker or anything and the fact that we met up in Japan is just weird, but I've seen you before."

"Where … when?"

"In San Francisco. I saw you in the gallery when you bought my painting and then on the news leaving the hospital."

Emily looked at him with a strange expression on her face. "I was in the hospital a couple of times recently, but I haven't been in any galleries and I didn't buy any paintings."

"I know it was you," Josh said softly. "I saw the article about your family on Yahoo news, too. I am so sorry you had to go through all that. It must have been horrible. And I was this close to you when you bought my painting of the Golden Gate Bridge."

Looking puzzled, Emily shook her head. "I haven't bought any paintings. Honest. I've been a bit, ah, busy."

Joshua was confused. "I don't understand." Then he thought about seeing Emily in the airport. Twice. In two different areas. "You know how they say everyone has a twin somewhere, I guess I saw yours," he concluded.

"But I do." Her eyes widened. "Have a twin. I just found out that I do. I've never even met her. I didn't know where she was or anything. You saw her in Frisco?"

"Yes, just down the road from where I live, in the gallery that shows my work. You act very differently from her, but you look the same. Your eyes are a little different though. Your eyes are more of a silvery-blue where hers are a deeper blue . Does she know about you?"

"I think so, maybe. I think she just found out about me recently too. It's a long story," she sighed.

"Well, we've got a long ride ahead of us. Won't you tell me about it?"

Emily looked at Josh. His expression was serious and he seemed like he really wanted to know. It would be nice to talk to someone about everything, she mused. "Okay, but you've been warned! Most of it isn't very pleasant."

For the next two hours, Emily poured out the story of her life. Joshua listened, taking her hand somewhere along the way, just holding it. Although they sat squished together on the crowded bus, it was if they were the only two people there. The fact that the chances were that no one else could understand what she was saying made it almost easy for Emily to pour out her story.

When the bus pulled in at a village perched on the edge of a mountain, they wandered around for the twenty-minute rest stop. Climbing back aboard, they were two of only nine when the bus started up yet another curvy road up a mountain. The woman with the baby was joined by a couple of teenaged boys and a mother with two children.

When at last she stopped, drained, as if she'd run out of words, Josh wrapped his arm around her and gave her a hug. "There's just one more thing you need to know," Emily said, almost whispering. "I'm not really going to Mt Fuji. Have you ever heard of Aokigahara or Jukai?"

Joshua simply stared at Emily and then, slowly nodded. "I guess it is my turn, if you would like to hear my story."

Emily looked up at Josh, smiled, and said, "I guess it is the least I can do. And I want to know why you even know about the forest."

Josh found he was able to talk with Emily as he was never able to talk to anyone. Not his family, not Susi. He told her everything. She just sat and listened until he mentioned the journals from his grandmother and what she'd told him about his family.

"Joshua, my grandmother's name was Alice. She's the one who left me the diary I told you about. She's the one who told me about Emma. Is she, my grandmother, your grandmother too?"

"I think so, but she's not really my grandmother, only through my mother's marriage to her son. This is really, really weird."

"It is. I didn't know about you from the journals. All mine talked about was me and Emma."

"I bet she'd be happy that we met though," smiled Josh. He felt a little strange as he continued on with his story, but, instinctively, he knew he could tell Emily what he'd never told anyone before.

He told her everything. He told her about his painting her picture and showed the photo he'd taken of it on his phone. Then, backing up the story a bit, he told her about the Yūrei.

"And then she said, 'You cannot do this here. You cannot do this now.' "

Emily, her face having grown several shades whiter, finished, " 'You must journey to Aokigahara.' "

Just then, a shiny blue car shot past them, causing the bus to swerve violently, crossing first to the right where the front bumper slid into the rocks lining the roadway, and then to the left and down over the embankment.

Chapter 21

Jinn was getting really tired of following the slow, creaky old bus up the curving mountain road. She'd been stuck behind it for miles, through hairpin curves and switchbacks as the narrow road snaked its way up through the low mountains. Every time the road opened up just a little, it seemed that there was always traffic coming the other way.

The far side of the road snugged up against sheer rock walls, and on her side of the car only a low rock wall stood between her and the valleys below. Once, she'd almost forgotten and tried to pass on the left rather than the right. Finally, she thought she had enough space, put her foot firmly down on the gas and shot through, only to have to cut over sharply as she saw another vehicle a short distance away. She pulled back into her lane right in front of the decrepit VW bus. Jinn sped on up the mountain, never looking back.

The VW bus slammed right through the low rock wall and slid down the embankment. The driver fought to keep the bus upright and bring it to a stop, but it just picked up momentum. Finally it hit a large boulder, careened off sideways and tilted up on two wheels. It continued moving, balanced for a moment or two and then, sliding down through grass and brush, it gave way to gravity and rolled several times before sliding into a swiftly running creek at the bottom of the hill.

Joshua came to lying in a tangle of arms, legs and baskets. His head was lying on something wet and sticky. He opened his eyes and saw red. He jerked his head up, and winced at the sharp pain in his neck. His head hurt too and someone was lying across his back.

He pushed himself up, never realizing he was pushing on someone else's body. He looked around, but nothing made any sense. It seemed as if he were lying on the roof of the bus. *Emily!*

"Emily! Emily, where are you?"

"Here," came a soft whimper. "Here, Josh," she repeated. She sat up, staring at the baby lying half in, half out of the water that was now a few inches deep. "The baby, someone get the baby!" Emily's voice rose to a shriek.

"We need to get out of the bus," his voice, calm, but insistent was just behind her. "Emily, can you walk? Are you hurt?"

"I think I can move, yeah, I'm okay, I think." She watched as a woman picked up the baby that still wasn't crying ...or moving.

Josh found their backpacks and helped Emily climb out of the window. Turning, each of them offered a helping hand to the children now climbing through the window. They sat down in the grass a little distance away from the overturned bus. Emily heard a high-pitched wail and thought, at first, it was the baby screaming. Then, she realized it was sirens as rescue vehicles wailed their way up the mountain.

Police climbed down to start assessing the damage and help those who were able to climb back up to the road. Joshua and Emily helped each other climb up the steep hill. Two men passed them carrying a stretcher. Back up on the road, a woman led them to an ambulance and checked them both over. Both were handed ice packs, and a tech cleaned up a scrape on Josh's leg.

More people made it back to the roadway. She saw the mother

with her two children and one of the teenage boys carrying the now squirming baby. Emily saw two men carrying a body bag between them.

Her legs folded beneath her and she collapsed into the dirt. "Joshua," she wailed. "We could have been killed! Those people are dead.."

"Shh, Em. We are okay. We're alive and barely even hurt. Shh now." He held her as she sobbed. However, her words rattled through his headache. Seemed like only moments earlier they'd been talking about Aokigahara and the Yūrei.

The walking wounded from the bus were given a ride to the next town. Checking in to the hotel, Emily tugged at Josh's arm.

"I don't want to stay by myself tonight."

He smiled, answering, "I really don't want to be alone either. One room?"

"Yes." Thanking the man for their room key, they walked up to their room and opened the door.

"I didn't think about asking for two beds," said Josh looking down at Emily.

"It's okay. I'm gonna take a shower." Grabbing her backpack, Emily went into the small bathroom, stripped off her clothes, turned the water on hot and then simply stood under the water. Tears streamed down her face as she stood there shaking. *Choices,* she thought. *I'm going to Jukai. My choice. I don't want that choice taken away from me. My choice. What I want.*

"Gonna leave me some hot water, Em?"

"Oh, sorry." She finished up quickly, climbed into some fresh clothes and opened the door.

Josh smiled and handed her a Pepsi. "Thought you might want this."

She smiled, opening the bottle and taking a long drink. "Thank you. I don't think a soda ever tasted so good!"

When Josh came out of the shower, the room was empty. Going outside, barefoot with his hair still damp, he found Emily sitting on a bench in the courtyard garden.

"Hey. You okay?"

"I guess. Strange day."

"Yeah. You tired?"

She nodded. "But I don't think I'm tired enough to sleep yet."

"Me neither."

They just sat there. Emily took his hand, rubbing her thumb over a deep purple bruise on his arm. "How's your head? Still hurting?"

"No, not really. Have a feeling we are both going to be sore tomorrow."

"Probably. Want to go for a bit of a walk? Feeling like I need to move about a little."

The moon had risen, It was full and its light cast a silvery glow on the small village. They walked the few blocks of the town and then around a curve where a stone wall enclosed a pasture.

They climbed over the wall and sat on the flat stones, their feet hanging. Joshua noticed some movement off in the middle of the field and pointed it out to Emily.

Speaking softly he whispered, "It looks like a flickering bunch of lights."

"It is someone dancing," she whispered back. "It looks like there are bits and pieces of mirror all over their clothing. It's the reflections of the moon we are seeing."

"It's beautiful," he murmured. "Just one person out dancing beneath the moon."

The man out in the field spun, arms outspread, head tilted back, his clothing catching and throwing moonbeams.

"It's like he's dancing for the stars or his gods. Dancing to music only he can hear," Emily said.

Now, he ran in larger circles, leaping, seeming to fly across the field. Then he slowed, walking as if in a stately procession. The he paused, brought his hands together in front of him and bowed.

"I almost feel as if we are intruding," she continued.

"Kind of like church or something. Serene, joyful."

"It's very special," Emily said leaning up against Josh. "I'm so very glad we saw this."

"We should get some rest."

Standing, they walked hand in hand back to their room. "Want me to sleep on the floor?" Josh asked.

"No, we can share. Weird, but I feel like I've known you forever."

They crawled into the bed and lay there looking at each other. Josh started to reach out to Emily, hesitated, and then reached over to brush her hair off her forehead. "You've got a bruise coming out here," and he rubbed his thumb gently over a bruise at her hairline.

"Does your shoulder hurt?"

"No, why?"

"Because I'd like to use it for a pillow."

Gesturing her over, he smiled. Emily edged over and rested her head on his shoulder, angled so that she could still see his face.

He looked at her, emotions conflicted. Then decided, the hell with it, and leaned down to kiss her. Gently, his lips just barely caressed hers. Her arms came up and her fingers twisted in his hair as her mouth opened beneath his. He opened his eyes to see hers looking deeply in his.

"I know we've just met, and this is crazy and …"

"I want you too."

"You know I will still go to Aokigahara. I still want to – to go there. This can't change that."

"I know. Me too. Kind of funny, though. For the first time in months my head isn't swirling with thoughts, it isn't jumping from one disconnected idea to the next. I am only thinking about one thing, Em. You."

With that, he brought his lips down to her forehead and then, gently to her eyes and then, once again to her lips. Her arms encircled him as she turned and, hungrily, kissed him back.

His hands gently skimmed down her body, artist's hands, feeling for texture and form. She was impossibly soft on the surface, but underneath the silken skin, she was lightly muscled. He loved how the light and shadow brought out her cheekbones, how her eyes went almost silver.

Her hands caressed the planes of his face. He looked like a poet with his long, choppy hair, his shadowed cheek, rough where it nuzzled her. His eyes were fathomless deep green pools, his lips gentle, then searching, seeking. She shrugged out of her tank top, lost her underwear in the covers as he teased her nipples taut, licking, nipping—and then soothing.

Heat built and words wafted away as he slid into her warmth. She arched to accept him, envelop him. Then, together they climbed, climbed higher until finally, they soared over the top of their own mountain. Neither heard the sound of the car screeching to a stop outside the room next to theirs, the angry slamming of the car door, or the drunken slur in her voice as a woman swore as she tripped going into her room.

Chapter 22

Jinn dreamed she was lost in a mirror maze at a carnival. Loud, disjointed chords from a calliope jangled as she searched for the way out. She saw herself coming and going, but the reflections were all wrong. The girl in the mirror had longer hair than she did and she wore different clothes. She turned and bounced off yet another mirror. Jinn tried to follow a pattern on the floor, searching for places where there was no seam, but kept getting tangled up. She kept seeing that other her. She spun around to see herself reflected again, and smiled until, behind herself, she saw the other reflection. Turning once again, she saw both reflections *ad nauseum*, over and over and over again. Putting her hands out, she reached and found herself completely boxed in...mirrors on all sides. She was trapped. Looking hard at her reflection that somehow wasn't a reflection, she saw minute differences, but she also saw how much alike the reflection and she were. Her twin moved when she did, grimaced as she did, but she wasn't Jinn.

"Go away," Jinn screamed. "You aren't me. I'm not you. I don't *want* a twin. I don't need some sister who gets everything. How are you better than I am? You aren't! You aren't! Go away."

She was flailing out now, her hands smashing into the

mirrors, and one gave way and she stumbled into another section of the maze — one where the mirrors distorted height and width. Now she saw herself and her twin with wildly contorted faces and bodies. Crying now, Jinn sobbed, "Go away!" and stopped in her tracks when the reflection, or was it a refraction of herself, answered her.

"Why do you think you are so special? You were the one given away. You were the one who was free. You didn't have to live my life. You had your own life, and I know it had to be better than mine."

"What?" Jinn gasped. "I was the one they didn't want."

"You were adopted by people who wanted a child, who wanted you. My parents wanted neither of us, but they ended up wishing they'd kept you. I wasn't what they wanted; I wasn't good enough at anything. Either way, my life was horrible. You didn't have to deal with Nick beating up you and your/our mother. You didn't have people walk out on you. You didn't have to be good enough for two." Jinn's reflection was now beating on her side of the glass.

"I – I- I'm sorry." Jinn turned around to see herself looking back at her. Tear stains ran mascara-ed rivulets down her face, her short hair spiked at odd angles. "I don't know what to say." She turned again, but her twin was no longer looking out at her. Jinn turned, but all the mirrors now showed Jinn, wild looking and panicked. "Emily! Where did you go? Emily, come back!"

Jinn spun around. She found a path and ran, checking all the mirrors as she ran, but now they showed only her. The music rose to a crescendo, chords all jangled together.

She awoke with Emily's name coming out of her mouth in an agonized scream.

Chapter 23

Joshua woke and stretched. His mind was blissfully empty and sleepy. Opening his eyes, he saw Emily curled in a ball, looking younger and smaller, like a child almost, but that changed the moment her eyes opened and she smiled.

"Good Morning."

"Hey you. How you feeling? Any stiff muscles?"

She uncurled and stretched, tentatively, and then fully. "Mmm. Nope. Not a one. Must have been all that, ah, exercise, last night helped." She grinned. "How 'bout you?"

"I'm good too. Need coffee. How about I go find us some?"

Emily smiled, answering, "Sounds really good. I feel really good. Last night was pretty amazing."

"It was, indeed." Josh grabbed his jeans, stepped into them and reached for his shirt. "Coffee. Necessary. Now."

"You are a man of few words in the morning, aren't you?"

"He nodded, repeating, "Coffee."

He'd reached the door when her voice stopped him.

"Joshua?"

"Hmmm?"

"Thank you."

"For what?"

"Last night. I really needed to..." Her voice trailed off.

Josh returned to the bed, sat down and cupped her chin. "I know. I did too. And you know what else? I'd really like to paint you the way you looked after, just as you were falling asleep, all tousled and cozy and looking very happy."

Emily blushed, grabbed a pillow and thwacked him with it. "Coffee. Now." She ordered. Josh was still grinning when he reached the coffee shop and realized he was barefoot.

Twenty minutes later, they sat on the bed, holding half-empty coffee cups and looking at the crumbs from their breakfast of croissants scattered across the blankets.

"So," Emily started, hesitantly. "What now? What next?"

Josh just looked at her, a frown forming a crease between his eyes. "I don't know. I mean I want. I need to go to..." His voice trailed off, his expression somewhere between lost and determined.

"Yeah. Me too. So you just want to work our way to Aokigahara, then? Maybe see some of Japan along the way?"

"Sure. It's not as if we are on a set schedule or anything. One day at a time, right?"

"Yeah. That will work. So, maybe we can rent a car or something?"

"Sure." Suddenly, Josh cracked a grin. "We sure are a pair, aren't we?"

Emily smiled. "Onward, then. North to Jukai!"

An hour or so later, Emily looked over as Josh drove. He had a puzzled look on his face.

"What is it? You look a million miles away."

"I was thinking. Why you and me? Why did Minami come see us?"

"I don't know," Emily replied thoughtfully. "I never even thought about it. Why did she, I wonder."

"It isn't like we are anything special ..." he continued. "Well, we are but, you know what I mean."

"Maybe it is like when people escape a plane crash or why there's a disaster and some live and some die. It just works out that way."

"So, you don't think it is because there's something special we are meant to do or something like that?"

She shrugged. "I guess we could ask her if we see her again. I'm glad she came to us, even though, well, you know..." Emily just stopped talking.

"Yeah, me too. Really hard to try and explain it to someone who didn't 'get' what's happening to us. Come to think of it, have you ever tried to talk to anyone about what we are planning to do?"

"No. I figured they'd lock me up in the psycho ward at the nearest hospital."

"Yeah. Got to be crazy, right?"

"We aren't crazy," she giggled. "We just talk to Yūreis."

"It is nice to be able to talk about these feelings, though. Haven't been able to do that before now."

"It is," she agreed.

Two hours later, they pulled the ancient Mitsubishi over and parked in a small town that clung to a cliff alongside the ocean.

There were people everywhere and, as they wandered through town, they saw a flier printed in both English and Japanese. It described a combination hang-gliding/hot air balloon/parachute celebration a few miles up the road that would be going on over the next two days.

"That might be fun to check out. Ever been?" asked Josh.

"No, not me. Planes are bad enough. Might be fun to watch though. I've seen hot air balloons over the Bay before; they looked kind of pretty against the sky. I always wondered what would happen if they got too far out over the water."

"Yeah, I always wondered about people who'd jump out of perfectly good airplanes!"

Emily giggled. "Maybe they've got a death wish!"

Josh laughed. Framing Emily's face, he kissed her as she laughed along. "If only I'd met you before, a long time ago."

"Yes, maybe things would be different. But we didn't, Josh, and all this," she motioned back and forth between them with her hand, "this is all just kind of a meantime thing. You know as well as I do, that it doesn't really mean anything. Not like everything else does." Her expression changed and she looked down at the ground. Then looking up, she continued. "It doesn't change a thing. It doesn't. It can't."

"I know, but..." his voice trailed off.

"Josh," her voice gentle now, "let's go watch the hang gliders and the parachutes. Let's watch balloons rise into a sunset. It'll be fun. A memory."

"Okay, I guess. Em? Why are we having good things happen now?"

"I don't know, but I sort of don't trust them."

Josh sighed, and holding hands, they hiked back to the car.

The following morning found Joshua and Emily with a crowd of people watching as the dawn flight of hot air balloons rose slowly in the cool morning air. Like grey ghosts, the balloons drifted upwards, their roaring burners spewing forth golden flames, the only color in the dimly lit sky.

The sun's rays didn't really catch the balloons until they had risen to a few hundred feet off the valley floor. Then, as the morning sun caught their bright colors, the sky seemed full of jewels. Rising to the heavens, they wafted quietly, wave after wave, until a veritable rainbow, hundreds of balloons thick, dotted the clear blue sky.

Emily lay in the grass, her head resting on Josh's stomach as they watched the spectacle above them. "It's like silent fireworks," she said in a hush voice.

"A palette of paint tossed against the sky," he whispered back.

"There's a poem floating around in those words," Emily answered.

"There is," said Josh, rolling over to reach for his notebook, as Emily, suddenly pillow-less, rolled too.

"It is almost too beautiful for words," she mused. "Feels like there should be music soaring and wafting in the breeze. A whole orchestra of violins singing."

They looked at each other and grinned. Then Josh dug deeper in his pack looking for a pen.

Chapter 24

Five miles away at the small, local airfield, the jumpers were in a registration line giving the officials their jump papers and paying the fee for the group jump that would happen a few hours later at 11:00 A.M.

Jinn stood with some new friends she'd met the night before. Fellow jumpers from both sides of the US, as they'd all done double-star jumps before, they'd quickly formed a group. They'd already sorted out who would take which position, who'd be the two middles, and what their jump order should be. They did several walk-throughs on the ground.

"We hold 'til 2500, then release. Everyone clear?"

Everyone answered in the affirmative. "Piece of cake," was Jinn's reply. She'd rather hoped they'd opt for the inverted star, but this was almost as good.

Although Jinn hadn't brought her own chute as some of the others had, she'd been able to rent equipment in the small village just beyond the airfield.

"I haven't jumped a chute I didn't pack in years," she said to Jimmy, a tall, lanky man with blond braids halfway down his back.

"No big," he replied. "Ya gotta take a few chances in this life, so you know you are alive, right?"

"I guess," she said.

"What, you aren't backing out on us, now, are ya? We got our doub-s going here. We need ya."

"No, I'm in," she smiled. "Check it out!" she said pointing up at the balloons high overhead. "There's something I've always wanted to do."

"Give me my chute anytime over one of those gasbags waiting for ignition," chimed in Daz, another member of the new group. "You couldn't pay me to go up in one of them," he said adamantly.

"Yeah," Jimmy agreed. "I like having my chute, or an airfoil. Those you can control. A stray spark and poof...crispy critter coming down hard!"

"I suppose," Jinn said quietly, "but still, it looks pretty peaceful right now."

"I like the rush from jumping. The wind in your face, feeling like you're flying while we make the formations. Nothing like it!"

"I guess, it would be different, is all."

"Not for this kid!"

"Me neither," the others in their group agreed.

A man with a clipboard came up to their group, once they'd been through the registration line.

"You're the American group, right?"

"Yes, sir." Jimmy answered.

"Okay then. You guys are in Group 4. You got the doub-star down; you've all done it before together, right?"

"Yeah," everyone answered in one voice.

"You'll take off in plane 31-Charlie at 11:23. Your LZ is the big green square marked 55. The guys from Group 3 will be all down before you take off. Any problems, forget the star, just land in one piece. No hot jumping, got it?"

Everyone nodded. "Safe landings then," he said as he went over to the next group.

"You're good, right?" Daz tapped Jinn on the shoulder.

"Sure am," she smiled. "We're getting quite the crowd to watch," she said pointing to a nearby hillside where folks sat in lawn chairs or on blankets in front of a couple of full wooden bleachers. "They don't give much room for misses."

"You know what Charlie Purcell says," he said smiling.

"Don't we all!" They recited in unison: " 'Out of 10,000 feet of fall, always remember that the last half inch hurts the most.' "

"It's a good day to jump," Daz said.

Jinn looked out at the various groups forming. She saw the guy she'd met on the plane and waved. She figured he didn't see her in the crowd when he didn't wave back.

Two hours later as the Cessna rose to the jump altitude of 6500 feet, Group 4 went over their dive plan again. Out, link, form, spiral away at 3000 feet. Jinn felt that feeling in the pit of her stomach she always did before a jump. She knew that the apprehension was normal, but it always caught her a bit by surprise. *You'd think I'd be over it by now,* she thought, but she knew better. When you quit being a little bit scared, it was time to quit jumping.

She was looking forward, actually, to the adrenaline rush, to the exhilaration that always came with the jump. She'd never been able to describe the feeling; either you got it or you didn't. It was as simple as that. All she knew was that there was no other feeling exactly like it in the world.

Third out the door, she hit the wind and flew. People always thought it would be quiet, but it was anything but. The air rushing past her jumpsuit was a low roar. Finding the others, she cut away to slide left. Her arms and feet spread-eagled, she shifted slightly and eased into position. Just as in other times, she felt as if she were moving in slow motion, although she knew she wasn't. Grabbing Jimmy's wrist, she felt, rather than saw, Daz grab her left arm.

Spiraling slowly to the left, they plummeted down, holding the formation. Lifting her head, she saw the others in the formation all had the same awe-struck expression on their faces. There was no being the 'nonchalant, jaded jumper' crap here. They all lived for exactly this; the rush, the exuberance, the thrill, the sheer joy of it all.

She was counting, as she knew the others were, as they looked down, finding the LZ below. At 3500 they broke, each diver continuing the spiral as they shot away from each other so their parachutes could open without fouling the lines of the others.

Jinn pulled the cord and looked up to see her green and white shoot billow up and then open. But it didn't feel quite right. It was catching the air, but she was spinning more than she should be. Often she'd spin and then unspin, like a child on a swing, but this was different. Her whole chute was spinning.

Not good. Not good at all. Jinn tried to compensate. She checked her altimeter and realized that she had mere seconds to fix it. Shaking her head, she pulled the release cord so she could deploy her reserve chute, but aside from a click, nothing happened. She pulled again. Again. Staring at the sky above her, she finally realized she was falling back first. Rolling over, she pulled her reserve chute again. Nothing.

"I am not dying today!" she screamed to the heavens.

Below her, the ground was getting way too close. She reached up with both hands and pulled as hard as she could. Click.

The force of her body being yanked upwards physically hurt, but her reserve chute was finally open. Her relief was short lived, however as she realized, looking briefly at her altimeter, that she was just under 800 feet and falling far too fast.

She'd done all she could do. "Emily," she murmured. "Guess I won't be meeting you after all."

The ground was rushing towards her; she was way off the drop zone and perilously close to the stands below. She could see people leaping off the bleachers. There was a rush of color, excruciating pain and then darkness.

Chapter 25

The next morning, Josh came running into their hotel room. It had been a very long night as both he and Emily had been upset after seeing one of the parachutes come crashing to the ground when the reserve chute opened only mere seconds before. They'd been in the jumble of bodies rushing off the bleachers. Emily had been very upset and, as a result, had had nightmares all night long. Although the girl wasn't killed when she landed, it had been a scary thing to watch.

"Emily, wake up! You need to see this."

Her eyes opened. Josh's face was bone white. "Wha- what's the matter?"

"This." he said, shoving the local paper towards her. "I went out for coffee and everybody in the restaurant was talking about it. The girl who crashed."

Emily took the paper Josh was holding out to her. The headline was in Japanese, but the picture needed no translation. She might as well have been looking in the mirror.

"It says her name is Jinn Lampon. I thought your sister's name was Emma," Josh said.

"That's what grandma called her, but I suppose her parents might have given her a different name. Where is she? Is she alive?

We have to go see her."

"She's at the hospital in town. Let's go!"

When they reached the hospital, Emily rushed to the information desk and showed the aide the newspaper.

"She's my sister. I need to see her. Where is she? How is she?" Emily's words came out in a rush. The woman gestured to a man walking by and spoke to him in Japanese. He came over to the couple.

"I am Dr. Oi. May I help you?"

"She's my sister," Emily said with tears streaming down her face. "I have to see her. Where is she? How is she?" she repeated over and over.

Dr. Oi looked at the picture of the girl in the newspaper and then at Emily. There was no question that the girls were related.

"Stay right here, and let me check for you." The doctor hurried off, but returned in less than five minutes.

"She's in ICU. She's in critical condition with multiple, severe injuries. Are you the same blood type? She needs a transfusion."

"I-I don't know. Can you check? Can I see her?"

"Let's check your blood type first," he said as he led her down a long white hallway and into a small examining room. He took a blood sample, told them to stay put and brought the sample to the lab. He returned shortly, smiling. "You are a perfect match. Not too many people have type O-negative blood and your sister needs a transfusion badly." He had her lie down and took a pint of blood from her.

"I want you to rest here for a bit and drink the juice the nurse is bringing for you. Then I will come take you to your sister. "

After the doctor left the room, Josh came closer to Emily and took her hand. "She's alive, Em. Are you ready for this?"

"I'm not sure. I have to be, I guess. I don't know what to say to her, but I have to see her."

"Kind of strange to see her for the first time like this. You realize, she might not be able to talk at all."

"I know," Emily said, softly. "Guess a lot of it will have to wait."

A quick knock and then the door opened. "Come with me," said Dr. Oi. "She's being given the transfusion, but you need to know that your sister is in very rough shape."

"I saw her fall," Emily said hesitantly. "I didn't know it was her though."

The doctor showed them to the first room on the right as they entered the ICU. It was like looking at herself lying there, although Jinn's hair was short and she was more bandage than skin. Both legs were in casts, as well as her left arm. IV bottles hung from supports on both sides of the bed. Numerous monitors chirped and beat in tune with her heartbeat. Emily's blood dripped into Jinn's arm. She had two black eyes and a large bruise on her forehead.

"She's awake, but not too responsive." He gently touched Jinn's shoulder. "Jinn, your sister is here to see you." He turned to Emily. "Only five minutes, understand? She needs rest more than anything."

"Jinn?" Emily began, "It's me, Emily. I thought I'd find you in California, not half a world away."

"Emily? As in twin? Guess we don't look much like each other at the moment." Jinn's voice was hoarse, and soft. "I'm pretty messed up."

"You just need to be okay," Emily responded.

"Why are you here? I mean in Japan. I came here so I wouldn't trip over you."

"Weird, isn't it? Long story as to why, but it'll keep."

A nurse poked her head into the room. "Okay, you two. Out. My patient needs her rest. You can come back in a few hours."

"We'll be right down the hall," Emily told her sister. "We'll be back as soon as they let us."

"Who's the we part of that?" Jinn asked groggily.

"My friend, Josh."

Jinn opened her eyes again. "Josh? As in Susi's Josh? Small world." Her eyes closed. The monitor beeped more rapidly.

"Now. Out." The nurse all but pushed them from the room. "You can wait down the hall there. Go."

Down the hall in a small waiting room, Josh and Emily did just that. They waited, sitting on hard, blue plastic chairs.

"She's got to be all right, Josh. I feel bad for all the things I thought about her. Our lives were no more her fault than they were mine."

"All we can do is wait, Em."

"Who's Susi?"

"She was my girlfriend. The one I told you about. All this time, your twin lived right down the hall from Susi. Never saw her around though. Susi used to talk about her friend, Jinn, all the time. She's really into extreme sports: hang gliding, parachuting, surfing.... If it scared the bejesus out of most folk, Jinn would try it. I vaguely remember Sus telling me about her name too. Her folks said she was their miracle child. She's always been like a genii, always taking chances and always coming out okay.

"This is all just too, too strange, Josh," Emily's voice was near tears.

Josh wrapped his arm around Emily as the tears overflowed and streamed down her face. Half an hour later, the nurse returned and said they should come.

"She's fading. We'd hoped the transfusion would help, but I think she's just lost too much blood."

"No." Emily looked at Josh with wide, scared eyes.

Emily rushed into Jinn's room and gently took the one hand that wasn't attached to wires or covered in bandages.

"I'm here, Jinn. Please, don't give up. We just found each other."

"I'm sorry." Her voice was barely above a whisper. "I'm glad you found me. I'm so lost ..."

"Jinn? Nurse!"

"She's okay, but she's unconscious again. Perhaps you'd better come back later. If you are going to stay at the hospital, I'll let you know when you can come back in."

"We'll be right here," Emily said softly.

Just then, another monitor started beeping, and the nurse shoved them out of the room.

"Josh? Oh no, Jinn?" Emily's voice rose to a shriek.

Finally, they were allowed back into the room. Now, with all the tubes gone and the beeping machines silenced, Jinn lay, tucked into the hospital bed, like a sleeping child. She looked smaller, somehow, than even her battered body had seemed hours earlier.

No, thought Emily, *not sleeping. She looks quietly dead. The essence, the spark was missing.*

"It seems so strange to be standing next to you and sort of s eeing you lying there," said Josh softly, taking her hand as if to prove to himself that his *(his?)* Em was still alive and breathing.

"I know," whispered Emily. "It is like looking at myself in a strange, distorted mirror." Dissolving in tears she continued, "It is just so sad, so terribly and utterly, sad to be saying a final goodbye less than three hours after we first said hello."

Chapter 26

After two sleepless nights and three days of arranging for Jinn's body to be cremated and sent to Reicliff back in California, Emily and Josh were once more on the road to Mt Fuji and Aokigahara. Emily was now fixed upon their destination.

They talked in the car on the journey north, but all Emily could focus on was the fact that she'd found her twin only to lose her. Her whole life she'd felt as if there was some indefinable 'something' missing, nothing concrete that she could identify, but something important. Now she'd figured out what it was, and it didn't matter because Jinn was dead. Everything seemed to center around that inescapable fact. Jinn was dead. Her twin. She didn't even know her yet; it wasn't fair. Emily felt as if half her soul had died with Jinn. She should be the dead one. She was the one who'd wished her sister had never been born. It wasn't fair. It wasn't right and there was absolutely nothing Emily could do about it. Except for one thing. She could join her sister in death. In life, they'd been separated, but in death, she could finally join her twin.

After a while, they sat in silence, the miles between them and their journey's end being eaten up as the road snaked before them.

Josh, he who had been aiming towards death his whole life,

couldn't talk her out of it. He, too, was spiraling out of control. He thought he might have found his reason to live, but now she was wanting to die as much, if not more, than he ever had.

He didn't understand the whole point of this journey he'd been more or less forced to take. What was the point? He felt numb. His mind jumped from one half-formed thought to another. Dazzling scenery passed before his unseeing eyes. Vistas that once would have compelled him to grab a pencil or a brush blurred, their colors washed away to shades of grey.

That night, curled up in bed together, they lay in each other's arms, but there might as well have been a continent between them.

Part of him wanted to reach out for Emily, to feel close to someone, something. Yet he felt as if a stone wall had risen up between them, and it was crushing him.

Emily lay there, barely breathing. Here she was lying in the arms of someone whom, in another life, she would have died to be with and… and…she started giggling. The giggling turned into gales of laughter.

"What?"

Emily only laughed harder. *How could she possibly explain? How could she tell him that here she was with the guy of her dreams and they both were on their way to Aokigahara and that it was completely ludicrous? It didn't make the slightest sense but it was what it was.* Her laughing was contagious, and soon, Josh was giggling too. He didn't know why, but thought perhaps, as laughter wasn't very different from crying – that maybe it was just a release. From a distance, it was difficult to tell crying from laughter after all. He wiped a tear from Emily's cheek. She brushed back the hair from his eyes and suddenly they were kissing.

Their lovemaking that night was frantic and furious. They rushed and devoured, strained and held on as if they'd never let go, until they did. Then they flew on until, depleted, they both collapsed against the thin mattress. Without saying a word, both slept. Yet in sleep, his arm tugged around her waist. Though deep in slumber, she curled into him. Above them, Minami's light flick-ered; a deep green flame, edged in pink.

Chapter 27

The next morning as they drove up the road to Shizuoka, Emily slumped against the door of their car staring out the window. She hadn't said a word since they'd awakened, hadn't bothered to brush her hair. She had just tossed her belongings into her pack and gone outside to wait for Josh. She watched the pines, straight and narrow, flash by like so many soldiers marching up a hill. Rain splattered on the windshield, the wipers keeping cadence with the pines. Lighting lit up the dreary sky off to her right, forking and slashing at the roiling grey clouds. It felt as though the skies were pressing down on her, like an unresolved argument. She sighed.

"What's the matter, Em? Thinking about your sister?"

She looked over at him, her eyes wet with tears she was determined wouldn't fall. "This thing," she began, "this thing between us: it doesn't change anything. It doesn't matter."

"Why doesn't it *matter?*" he asked, emphasizing the last word.

"Because it doesn't. It can't. Oh Josh, I'd just lose you too, like I lost my grandmother, my mom and now Jinn. I always lose whatever it is that is important to me. I lost the baby, I can't seem to hang on to a boyfriend, and nothing makes any sense anymore. Maybe I curse them or something. I don't know, I just know that I lose what I love—"

Josh started to interrupt, but hesitated at her last words. *Love? She loved him? Great timing.* Thinking about that and how he himself felt, he missed her next couple of sentences, but tuned in when he heard her sob.

"… It all just hurts so badly. Clear through. I just want to stop hurting."

"Em," he began helplessly. He knew the pain, the ebb and flow of the crushing pain, the manic waves that came one after the other in unrelenting onslaughts of agony.

Lightening burst across the sky, followed by a crack of thunder, sounding like an angry palm slapping an offender into submission. Emily shrank back against the seat, her face white beneath her freckles, which now stood out in stark relief.

"I just don't want to live this way. I don't want to die, but I can't live with this…I just ca-can't." And she broke down in gulping sobs.

Josh pulled off to the side of the road. He put the car into park and then turned to her. "I understand, Em. Truly I do. It's different for me, but I do understand. My thoughts whirl so fast, I get dizzy. The colors blur to nothing but muddy grey and my world dissolves into an icy cold mush. I can't find individual words; I can't find the right colors. Without the words, I can't write; without color, I can't paint. My emotions just go cold, empty. I pitch into a black hole where everything spirals down in an unending fall. I'm afraid to keep falling; I'm afraid to land and find nothing there. I want my brain to stop, go to sleep and never wake up."

He could sense she was listening, her sobs retreating to gulps of air. He saw her swipe her fist under her nose and kept talking. "But these last few days have been different. There were even times in the last few weeks, leading up to now, when it wasn't as bad. I had moments, hours when I could write – and, you saw the painting. Sometimes it is like there is a tiny light, far away to be sure, but sometimes I almost think that just may be…" His words trailed off.

"May be what? Maybe this is different? That maybe because that freakish Yūrei came on the scene that it changes everything? Really?" Her voice was cold and hard. Brittle. As if with just the slightest touch, she would crack and fall apart into so many slivers and shards that nothing could ever glue her together again.

"I don't know, Em, I don't. But it has been different," he continued stubbornly. Then, heaving a sigh himself, he muttered, "but you are probably right. Not different enough to matter."

He pulled back onto the road and continued into the city. "We need to get the ribbons," he said. "I read that it isn't a good idea to get them too close to Aokigahara. Too many questions neither of us want to answer."

Emily reached into her bag and bringing out her brush, ran it through her hair. She looked into the mirror on the backside of the sun visor. She looked tired and pale, but at least her hair looked reasonable.

"I wonder how much we need to get. I don't guess there is enough on a roll or two."

"We'll just buy a bunch and when we run out, we run out," he answered simply and pulled into an outlet shopping mall that almost made them both feel as if they were stateside. A sign read, 'Gotemba Premium Outlets.' They got out of the car and stood there looking beyond the mall. The rain had stopped and the clouds let rays of sunlight through, turning the snow on the peak of the volcano into burnished gold.

"Wow," Emily exclaimed, "I feel like we should be watching some old travelogue—'Beyond the red tiled roof of the mall, Mount Fuji dominated the skyline, rising majestically to command the sky!'"

"There ya go, you need a job on the Travel Channel on TV," Josh grinned. "Well, at least in one of these stores, we should be able to find some ribbon."

They wandered along, window-shopping as they looked for

the right kind of store. Stopping at one store that reminded them both of a Michael's store back home, Josh opened the door and they went in.

They found spools of ribbon near the back wall of the store, but none of them had anywhere near enough ribbon on them.

Emily approached a woman who was cutting cloth at a long table edged in meter sticks.

"Can I help you?" she asked in halting, but perfectly pronounced English.

"I need a lot of ribbon. Do you have bigger spools somewhere? What we've seen only have about ten yards, I mean meters, on them."

The woman's eyes narrowed, taking in the two twenty-something people in front of her. "What do you need it for?" she asked, her voice sounding both stern and worried.

"I, ah, need it for… for our wedding," Emily said, forcing a dazzling smile on her face. "I need lots and lots to decorate the tables and for the bouquets and…" her voice trailed off.

"Yellow and red," added Josh, as he also plastered a happy smile on his face and looked down at Emily. "She wants ribbons and bows on everything. Women" he said, shaking his head. "But that's what she wants, so that's what we get," he finished bravely.

"Your wedding?" the woman asked in a voice that didn't sound convinced. "When are you getting married?"

"Next week," Emily said in a rush. "At Lake Kawaguchi. We've so much to do before then."

"My mother said this was the best place to get ribbon if you needed a lot," added Josh.

"Well then, over here," she said walking a couple of aisles over. Her voice still didn't sound convinced, but after watching the two of them exclaim over the numerous shades of reds and yellows, and seeing them giggle and kiss, she shook her head, shrugged her shoulders and went back to her table.

They settled on two large spools of ribbon, bright spools of *Ki* (yellow) and a bright pinkish-red called *Kurenai*. Carrying them to the front of the store, checking out and returning to their car, they finally dissolved into the giggles that both had been holding back.

"For our wedding?" Josh chortled.

"I was the first thing I thought of! It worked, didn't it?"

"Sure did, just caught me a bit by surprise is all," he paused, "considering."

"I guess it is a bit ironic, but we have our ribbon. Why'd you say red and yellow?"

"You were wearing a bright yellow jacket when I saw you in the airport," he answered, "and I love that reddish pink of the sunset. Besides, I think I read somewhere that red is a wedding color here."

"Oh," she answered in a small voice. "They do look pretty together.

"I saw some daisies with those colors once. The petals were all yellow, but the middles were that bright reddish-pink."

"That's funny," Em said with a smile.

"Why?"

"Because a daisy is my favorite flower. They just seem so, I don't know, happy," she decided. "They grow everywhere, in odd, unexpected places and daisies always feel so free. I always thought that if I should ever get married, I'd want to carry daisies."

"Don't take this wrong, Em, but I can see that. I can picture you and an armful of daisies with that half-smile you smile."

Changing the subject, Emily suggested that they get back on the road, if they were going to get to the Kawaguchiko Station Inn before dark. "It won't be safe driving these mountainous roads after dark."

Josh just shook his head, smiled, and navigated their way to the 139 Line that would take them up and around Mt Fuji and into Kawaguchi.

A few hours later, they stopped to stretch their legs. To their right, the mountain loomed.

"It's easy to see why there are so many myths about Mt. Fuji," said Emily, gazing up at its peak.

"It is intimidating," added Josh. "I'd like to paint it someda—" he stopped and walked away a few steps. *No, you don't, you idiot. That's not why you came here!*

Emily edged over and ran her hand down Josh's arm. "It is hard, isn't it? Feeling somewhat torn, myself. But it is what I want to do. Right now, it is difficult, but I know that a few days, a week, or a month from now, everything would change yet again. I won't change my mind, Josh," she said seriously, looking up at him.

"Come on then, let's get to the hotel. We can turn in the car in the morning and take the bus to Aokigahara."

They both were silent the rest of the way to their hotel. Each drew in the coverings of their mind as if they were pulling up blankets. Yet both were discovering that these particular blankets didn't warm them at all. In the backseat, Minami floated serenely. It *was* a journey, after all.

Chapter 28

Neither of them said a word as they passed the signs pointing the way to Jukai and the Ice Caves. Each, still wrapped in a mantle of thoughts, stared with stony faces straight down the road in front of them.

They found the inn with little trouble, as it was just past the train station. They checked into their room and decided to wander about for a while and stretch their legs. When Josh pointed towards the Kawaguchiko train station, a building that reminded both of them of something they might see in Switzerland, they meandered in and then stopped in their tracks. Everywhere they looked were small mirrors. They were nailed to walls, hanging from thin chains, propped against windows and attached to the ceiling.

In them, were reflected all the people passing through the busy station. It was a swirling kaleidoscope of humanity, the bits and pieces of myriad lives dancing before them.

"I read somewhere that the Japanese believe if you can see yourself, then you exist. The hope is that someone on the way to the forest will catch his or her reflection and that maybe it will change his or her mind."

They wandered over to one of the vending machines, but

after looking at the odd contents, decided against buying anything. They settled onto a bench and sat for a while, just watching the people coming and going.

One woman in particular caught Emily's eye. She was an elderly woman, with long, long black hair streaked with grey. Her face was cracked and wrinkled like a crumpled piece of parchment, her eyes a hollow black. She looked infinitely tired and inexorably sad. She wore a long dark grey skirt, a black blouse and had on a sweater that was tattered with loose threads hanging. Her clogs were spattered with mud and, slung on her back, was a loosely tied bag. The bulge in the bag reminded Emily of the spools of ribbon they'd bought. She shook her head in denial.

"Em, look." Josh pointed upwards and in front of the very woman at whom Emily had been staring. "Maybe it's our angle, but I don't see her reflection in any of the mirrors, do you?"

"I need to get out of here." Emily took off at a run for the exit. She sprinted on past the old woman, trying to keep her eyes from all the mirrors. She looked down as she ran, but then realized there were even mirrors embedded into the floor. Just as she was about to go through the door leading outside, a green-ish flash in the mirror above the door caught her attention. She stopped dead in her tracks, and Josh slammed into her, not expecting her abrupt stop.

"I see us," she whispered.

"I do, too," he whispered back. "But I still don't see the old woman."

Chapter 29

Later that night, Emily's iPhone beeped its 'I need to be charged.' beep. She looked at it and answered Josh's questioning glance with, "I don't guess I need to worry about that any more. Kind of freeing, actually. Look at all this stuff I brought with me. It is just that: stuff. Why'd I even bring it? Oh!" Emily looked over at Josh and then back at their bags. "Our stuff? What do we do with it? I didn't think about that!"

"I did," Josh answered. "When I rented the room, I had to rent it for three days. Some hotel rule or something. We can leave it here. By the time they figure out we aren't coming back, it won't matter," he continued softly.

"Oh," she replied sounding almost disconcerted. "So. What do people do on the last night of their lives?"

Josh shook his head. "I don't know, really. At some point, I want to do some writing. Maybe I need to leave something behind. I might not finish it until we get," he paused for a second, "there. I'm not sure what I want to write, but I need to write something."

"Yeah, I was planning on bringing my journal with me too. Josh," she stopped and took a deep breath, "what's your favorite memory?"

He looked thoughtful for so long, Emily was afraid that he wasn't going to answer at all.

"Favorite is an odd word. Favorite because it made me happy or favorite because it felt huge, important, life changing? To be brutally honest, my favorite moments might seem selfish, petty or mean. I think they were more defining moments rather than the 'Christmas I got my first bike' moments. They were instances when I felt free, really free, and not the feelings most people would expect someone to feel at those moments."

"I'm not most people, Josh."

"I know that, Em." He took in a huge gulp of air. "Take when the towers fell on 9/11. My dad, or who I thought was my dad at the time, was on the 89th floor. He never stood a chance. I was horrified by the idea that they'd crash planes into the building. I hated the fact that I knew there'd be so many people who wouldn't make it out alive. Good people. Loving people. People who had never seriously hurt another human being in their entire lives. People that didn't deserve to die like that.

"But I remember thinking that Dad was never coming home again. Emily, I was happy! People saw me in tears and tried to comfort me. They did the normal, human things to help. I let them, because while I celebrated on the inside, I had to be someone else on the outside that people could see. I hid what I was really feeling beneath the mask of a grieving son. I couldn't fake that for very long, so I moved out the next day. For the first time in my life, I felt free to be myself. I would never feel the heel of his hand pushing me into the dirt ever again.

"I could be who and what I wanted to be. Of course, Boy 1 and Boy 2 had a lot to say about that and my sisters weren't any better. I'd never be good enough, strong enough, smart enough or anything enough for their misguided ideas of what was barely acceptable. But none of that mattered. They couldn't hurt me any more. My life might not have been all that great, and yes, I still had problems, but I could paint. I could come and go as I pleased, and I was responsible for no one and nothing but myself.

"Honestly? If he'd been alive when I found out that self-righteous son of a bitch hadn't been my dad after all, I don't know what I'd have done. All those years when he put me down, when he compared me to the Boys and I was always found lacking. When no matter how hard I tried, no matter how hard I fought, no matter how much I studied—it just didn't matter to him. Stupid me. I always thought I was disappointing him. I was older. I should have been better. But, Em, he wasn't disappointed. Hell no. He was gloating. He was so fricking happy that *his* boys were better at everything. He might have been stuck with me, but his sons were real sons, real men. And me? I was just left-overs, worthless garbage that should have been thrown out with the trash."

Wound down and worn out, Josh stopped talking, yelling really, and looked over to Emily who was sitting cross-legged on the tatami.

"Wow. Oh, Josh." Her voice trailed off sadly. "Yeah, I was going for a bike moment. Mine was getting twin dolls one Christmas. I loved those dolls. I dressed them the same, fixed their hair the same. I named them Veronica and Victoria. Pretty lame joke on their parts, wasn't it? Looking back, I remember wanting a sister so badly. I thought being half a set of twins was the coolest thing imaginable.

"Funny, isn't it? Looking back, even our 'good' moments were turned by the events that made us who we are. It is like looking back through an album, but it is only the photographic negatives pasted in there. I know Grandma Alice meant well, but sometimes… sometimes it is as if her letters drained all the color out of our lives."

"We are a mess, aren't we?" Josh asked, coming over to sit next to Emily. "But I'm glad she wrote those letters. They explained so much, even if they raised questions we can't answer. She wanted us to know the truth, Em. Even if the truth sucks.

"Oh Em, I am so torn. Part of me wants to, really wants to

prove to every one of them that they were wrong, but most of me just can't deal with it, doesn't want to deal with all the different ways to look at things. It is like when I paint, it is my choice to choose the colors, add the various shadings to the pictures. *They've* mixed the colors all together, broke all the brushes and left us muddy water."

"Our ribbons are pure color," she said quietly. "They can't take that away."

No, but we will, Josh thought. *Or will we? Those ribbons will still be flashes of brightness, long after we are grey shards of bone.*

Emily pulled Josh into an embrace. "I really want tonight to be about the one good thing in my life. Even if it is just for a few moments, I need that brightness, that color. I know it may not make any sense, Josh, but I really need that."

Josh looked deep into her eyes. "I have a few things I need to do first. We need to figure out what we are bringing with us and what we are leaving here. In the morning, I just want to be able to leave, okay?"

She nodded. Going through her backpack, she set out the clothes she'd wear in the morning. She picked up the yellow jacket she'd worn to the airport and decided she'd wear that too. She tucked her medication into the jacket pocket.

"Josh," she paused. "How are you going to… going to…"

"How am I gonna do it? I've got my pills with me. I don't want to fight the going. I just want to go to sleep and never wake up."

He paused. "Um…Emily, there's something else I need to tell you. I need to do this by myself. It's important to me to take my final steps alone. I want us to go separate ways once we are in the forest."

"Yeah, okay." Emily looked down at her lap. Somehow, in all of this, she'd figured they'd do it together. He had a point, though. She needed to finish this on her own, by herself. "Yeah, I get that. Death is a private thing. It isn't something you can do together. When all is said and done, everyone dies alone." She smiled hesitantly.

She stretched out on her mat. She'd changed into a long t-shirt, and was waiting for Josh to finish writing in his journal. She was so tired. She slept.

In her dream, Emily wandered through one of Josh's paintings. A couple of days ago when they'd been eating at a restaurant with Wi-Fi, he'd shown her the gallery's website and his paintings that currently were there. Her favorite had been one painted down at the shore. The sky was a pale blue wash, but the sea was full of angry waves pounding, pounding the sand and rocks. She was on a cliff, above the painting. Then she saw Jinn sitting on a rock, her face raised to the sun.

"Jinn!" *What was she doing here? She was dead.*

"I waited for you. We had so little time. I thought we could soar together." Jinn pointed to a hang glider resting at the edge of the cliff. "It is such an amazing experience, so free. I feel like I'm flying."

Emily shook her head. "No, I couldn't. It is so dangerous."

"Kind of late to be worrying about dangerous now, isn't it?"

"But, that's not how ..." Emily's voice trailed off. "Let's walk instead."

Jinn stood and the two of them were suddenly walking down a hall of mirrors. "This," Jinn waved her hand, "is like the Hall of Mirrors at Versailles. Ever been?"

"Yes, but this isn't anything like that. They were all golden and shiny. These are tarnished, and look," Emily brushed a hand over the frame. "It's all crumbling gilt just painted on and the mirrors are all spotted and wearing away."

"It is all how you look at it," responded Jinn. "Look at us, instead."

Emily looked into the mirror and saw herself and her twin. Behind them, she saw themselves reflected in the other mirrors again and again. Yet she saw their faces too. Over and over and over.

"I never wanted to die, you know," Jinn began. "I loved the rush of the danger, but I never wanted to die. Living was such a kick. Even after I read the journals, I wanted to live. I wasn't sure I ever wanted to find you, but I would have. I know I would because finding you would have been one more rush, one more layer of color. I just wasn't ready then. I wish I had been."

"We'll be together soon."

"No," Jinn countered. "We won't. We will still have to search for each other. We won't," she paused, "we won't look the same any longer. I can't explain it."

Suddenly, Jinn was gone. All Emily could see were reflections of herself, refractions of who she was, of what she'd been and could have been. "Jinn, Jinn!" she called, but there was no answer. She ran down the long, darkening hallway and burst out into the light of the cliff face.

The hang glider was still on the edge of the cliff, its wings flapping in the breeze. Emily saw a faint outline of her sister as the glider took flight, and heard the sound of thrilled laughter on the edges of the wind. Then it was gone, lost in ribbons of stardust in space and the blaze of sunlight on golden water.

Chapter 30

Emily awoke in the middle of the night. Josh's arm cuddled her close. The misty fragments of her dream still swirled in her head, but she was quickly distracted from them when Josh nuzzled her neck.

"Need you," he murmured softly. "Need to make love one last time. I need to have you to take with me."

His hand roamed from the side of her face, down her torso and under the t-shirt that had hiked up in her sleep. Before she was even totally awake, she found herself responding to his now fevered kisses.

"Need you, too," she whispered through his kiss. Their touches were gentle now, not grasping as they'd been the last time they'd made love. In each of their minds was the thought that this was the last time they'd ever do this, the last time they'd reach out in need or love to pull another close, to open themselves up to a nother human being.

His fingers reached down to cup her, and she arched against his hand. Just his touch was enough to send her spinning through the vortex, yet before she'd even crested the top, he had slid into her. Together they rode the wave. Emily had a quick flash of golden waters and the feeling she was flying before they both flew up and over.

"Nice," she mumbled through his shoulder.

"Uh-huh," he said, barely tumbling off to her side before sleep overcame him. Emily's last conscious thoughts were that they hadn't used anything, but that it didn't matter.

A few hours later, they both woke to sun streaming in the windows and neither of them feeling as if they'd slept at all. Josh made the coffee the hotel provided, and they sat, not talking, as they drank it. Without saying a word, both of them dressed and gathered what they were taking with them. Each had a backpack loaded with a spool of ribbon and the appropriate personal journal. Finally, Josh broke the weighted silence.

"Well, I guess we should go. The bus comes at 10:00."

Emily nodded and together, they left their room.

The bus was crowded with tourists eager to see the ice caves at Aokigahara. Emily and Josh ended up sitting several seats away from each other, as only single seats were left. That was okay with Emily, because she felt herself shrinking away from contact with anyone at all. Yet she noticed that three seats ahead of her was the same old woman they'd seen the day before in the train station.

The ride took about half an hour and Emily linked up with Josh as they got off the bus.

"Did you see her?"

"See who?" asked Josh.

"The lady from the train station. See?" Emily pointed ahead as the fifteen or so people wended their way into the cave.

"She is taking the trail. She isn't going in."

Josh looked where Emily pointed and saw the old woman walking slowly along the trail. They watched her as the trail curved and she was out of sight.

"Do you think she's going to…"

"Yeah, maybe."

Emily shivered. "Kinda creepy, in a way."

"And we aren't?" asked Josh as he shouldered his knapsack.

Emily shrugged.

They walked past the point where people were veering off into the ice cave and, instead, followed the trail. Up ahead they could see where the path forked, but one of the forks was roped off. They stopped and watched the old woman put down her bag, pull a spool of blue ribbon from it and tie the end to a tree. Then, holding the spool in her hands, and slinging her bag over her shoulder, she stepped around the barrier and disappeared into the forest.

"Guess maybe we should give her some time so she doesn't feel as if we are following her."

"I guess," Emily answered. "It is pretty here, in a dark sort of way. Listen. No birds. It is so quiet in here."

They walked slowly up to the barrier and silently read the sign that was posted on a banner attached to the rope.

あなたの人生はあなたの親からの貴重な贈り物です。ご両親、兄弟姉妹や子供とお考え下さい。自分自身にそれを維持しないでください。あなたの悩み（助けを得るだけでは、この通過しないでください）について話しています。自殺予防協会への連絡

'Your life is a precious gift from your parents. Please think about your parents, siblings and children. Don't keep it to yourself. Talk about your troubles (or 'Please get help, don't go through this alone). Contact the Suicide Prevention Association 0555 – 22 – 0110

Looking solemnly at each other for a moment, they stepped beyond the barrier, and walked down the trail.

Chapter 31

Minami wafted along the trail, unseen, just above the top branches of the closely growing trees. She followed not only Josh and Emily, but also the hunched over figure of the aged woman who was walking slowly down the path.

The feelings that surged through Minami were strange to her. For so long, she'd simply floated, emotionless, a shadow of the young vibrant woman she'd once been. Ever since she'd been sent by some unknown force across the oceans to interact with Josh and Emily, she'd felt their return. Slowly at first. A ripple of urgency, a rush of joy, a frisson of anger, a sense of helplessness. It had been so long, just *how* long, she wasn't sure, since she'd felt anything at all.

Thus, she really wasn't sure quite *what* she felt upon watching her sister walk towards her destiny. A very long time ago she might have felt a sense of retribution. She might have felt her sister had gotten no more than she deserved.

Minami risked a brief link with her sister's mind. In those brief seconds, she saw a multitude of images, fleeting wisps of anger at a man who'd betrayed her, of a sad, lonely woman whom no one loved and who no longer loved anyone, of desperate unhappiness, of a female child left to die on a hillside. Pity,

Minami decided. What she felt was pity, and an unbearable sadness. Somewhere along the way, the hate, the being unable or unwilling to forgive had faded. In seeing the wretched ghost of the living woman, Minami felt only a sadness for what had been lost and what, now, could never be.

To think that she, who had tried so hard to guide Josh and Emily away from what this place had come to represent, would be here, now, at the precise time her sister would do exactly what she still prayed Emily and Josh would not. She couldn't reach out and communicate with her twin. She knew that. Nevertheless, a part of her wished she could let her know that she no longer harbored any ill feelings towards her. This was a journey her sister had begun long ago and Minami was powerless to do anything about it.

She also realized that with her sister's death, she would have very little time to interact even a final time with Josh and Emily. She knew she would be in this world only for a short while after they reached whatever decisions they made. One way ... or, and she shuddered, the other.

Chapter 32

Emily reached over to take Josh's hand as they walked along the trail. They had passed where the old woman's ribbon left the trail and snaked off through the trees.

She could feel him withdrawing. She could feel herself pulling in, as if she were slowly wrapping an enveloping cloak around herself blocking everyone and everything else out. But, she wasn't quite ready to let go of everything. Not yet. She forced herself to speak. To say something. Anything.

"Josh?" she said in a questioning voice.

He looked over to her and stopped walking.

"It is so beautiful in an eerie sort of way. The phrase 'quiet as death' keeps swirling around in my mind. I had to say something. I needed to hear the sound of a voice."

He nodded. "You know that skeleton we passed a while back? I've been thinking about that. I couldn't ever hang myself. I had this image of a body hanging from a tree casting its shadow on the ground. I got to thinking how, as time went by, as it became nothing more than bones, how its shadow would change. How there'd be less and less of a shadow to be cast. Until it would leave no shadow at all. It made me so sad to think they wouldn't even leave a shadow behind."

Emily sighed. "What we are going to do is a big thing. Big to us, if no one else. You leave something concrete behind you, Josh. You will leave behind your words and your art."

"We won't die alone, either. I think we will bring pieces of the hearts of everyone we've ever known or loved to travel along with us. We might be physically alone, but our minds carry the others right along with us whether we want to bring them or not. Emily, I want you to know, you are the one good piece I will bring with me."

"I don't know what to say right now. I feel as if I should say something momentous or worthwhile or earth-shattering."

Josh smiled and opened his pack. "I drew this last night while you were sleeping. I thought you might like to have it. I drew one for me as well."

He handed her a folded piece of paper. "Don't open it now. Open it when … well, open it later."

She smiled wistfully. "Please know that these last days have mattered." Saying that, Emily took her spool of yellow ribbon out of her bag and tied the end to a tree on one side of the trail. She reached up and framing his face with both hands, sweetly kissed him one last time. Then she picked up her backpack, slung it over her shoulder, and letting the ribbon spool out behind her, stepped off the path and headed into the forest weaving her way between the thickly growing trees. After only a few moments, she was lost from Josh's sight. The only thing left behind, was a trail of golden ribbon.

Chapter 33

Josh removed his ribbon from his bag and tied the end to a tree on the other side of the track. The loose end fluttered and then fell limp, a slash of red belying life. He headed off in the opposite direction from the one Emily had taken.

He wandered for a while, his mind lost. He tripped over a knobby-kneed root and fell hard. In front of his tear-blurred eyes was a pair of glasses someone else had left behind. *Was there nothing left to see,* he wondered? *Had the wearer no longer cared to look about him.? Had the eerie quiet unnerved the wearer or had he seen something that caused him to retreat into a blurred world?*

He walked for another few minutes or so, weaving in and around the trees, stopping occasionally, lost in thought. He wandered past places where the roots twisted and turned, wrapping around tree trunks to form sinuous patterns. He came to a clearing and was ready to stop, when he saw the frayed and knotted twist of rope hanging from a branch, the loose fibers gray from weather and time. He moved on, unwilling to infringe on another's chosen spot. Perhaps twenty feet further along he saw a blaze of yellow cut through the thick canopy overhead and came to a mossy knoll. Setting down his pack, he realized he'd come to the end of his ribbon. *End of the line, old pal,* Josh thought as he dropped the empty spool. How many feet had he wandered? How many feet away from life. Mere inches and a couple of chugs of water to go.

He sat down next to an especially gnarled and twisted tree trunk, opened his bag and removed his journal, his last bottle of water and the almost full bottle of pills.

He thought about what he was planning to do, what had led him to this point. This journey. *Where was the Yūrei now? I've made the journey to Jukai: I came to Aokigahara. Now what?*

Josh reached into his pack again and took out the drawing he'd done of Emily and thoughtfully unfolded it.

He'd captured her in an unguarded moment, sweetly asleep. She lay curled on her side, but relaxed rather than the tense way she always seemed to sleep. There was an odd little half smile on her face and her tawny brown hair lay in curled wisps framing her face.

Even with the destination of this journey looming over them, they had developed a relationship that, thinking about it, Josh wasn't completely convinced he wanted to give up. Something about her let him relax, made the spirals slow down. He could think and focus around her, and that, Josh thought, was so odd. Hadn't been that way around Sus. She'd almost fed into the manic tenseness he often felt.

What to do? In a matter of days, I've come to rely on Emily. I can really talk to her and I don't feel stupid doing it. She listens; she really listens to me. I've told her things I've never told anyone before. Why is that?

Josh ran his finger over Emily's face in the drawing. *What is it about her that lets me do that? If I weren't going to end it all here and now, would it really make a difference? Is that what Minami wanted me to figure out?*

Josh stood and paced around the small clearing. His eye caught some of the vivid green moss that was everywhere in the forest. It coated tree trunks, crawling up the sides of the trees as if straining for sunlight. He reached out one long finger to caress it. It felt soft, with an almost fluid feeling to the tiny fronds. *I feel whole around her. It's like, like … like she's the other half of my heart,* he thought. *Where did that come from? I can't love her. Can I? Do I? I sound like a character in some chick flick!*

He laughed. It rumbled up from his stomach and he stood there laughing 'til tears flowed down his face. Then the laughter turned into real tears as he sat with his head in his hands. *What am I doing? This is ridiculous.* "Enough already!" he said, his words shattering the silence.

Josh reached over and picked up the bottle of pills. He opened the cap and spilled five into his hand. He looked at the mixture of long white pills and round blue ones. The bottle was full between the two.

A Xanax and Lunesta cocktail…I can sleep my way to forever and not have to deal with anything ever again. Minami didn't make the bottle roll away this time. Is the fact that I'm here mean it is okay?

Josh uncapped the water bottle and was just about to toss back the first handful of pills when the thought struck him that he really did *not* want to do this.

Of course I do. I just traveled halfway across the world to do this. He raised his hand again, but then paused. *But what if…I didn't?* He looked once again at the picture of Emily. *Could he? Could they? Could Emily be the catalyst that allowed him to change? To get it together? Could he? Minami? Where are you when I want to talk to you? What would you tell me or would you just spout off one of your unanswerable riddles?*

"I'd tell you that you already know the answer, Joshua. People always think it takes strength to die. But your question is: are you strong enough to live?"

Minami floated serenely a few feet in front of Josh.

"I will tell you that you can do this here and you can do this now. I do not have the power to stop you any longer. Only you have that power. Only you can make that choice. What have you learned on your journey, Josh?"

Josh was silent for a moment, thinking. Then he remembered a conversation he and Emily had had.

"Minami, why us? Or do you 'talk' to bunches of other suicidal people too?"

"I cannot answer that, Joshua. I do not know the answer. You and Emily are the only ones I was driven to reach out to. I do not know if other Yūreis do or not as we cannot speak with each other. You and Emily are the only ones I've ever spoken to."

Minami flickered brightly for a moment. "I cannot stay with you. Make your decision, Joshua. One way or the other. I pray you make the right one."

Minami flickered again and then was gone. No flames marked her exit this time.

Josh thought for a moment about what Minami had said. *Strength. Am I strong enough? Where could Minami have gone? Emily!*

Minami must have gone to Emily. Suddenly the thought of Emily dying was more than he could bear. She couldn't die!

Josh was on his feet and running, following the ribbon as it twisted and turned through the trees. He tripped over an exposed root and fell flat on his face. He'd made his decision, he thought as he ran. He'd decided that regardless of what he had thought about and planned for, that Emily could not die. She couldn't.

Up and running again, his breath heaving in and out, he realized that it was more than just Emily. *I don't want to die. I don't want her to die. I need to get to her!*

Afraid he'd get lost if he followed his gut and just took off through the forest towards where he thought she'd headed, he stuck with the ribbon even though he realized he'd wandered in circles and not even realized it. *Nothing new there*, he thought ruefully. *I guess I've been doing that for years.*

Leaping over a fallen branch, he ran, his eyes hoping for the sight of that sunny yellow ribbon, even as he screamed out her name.

Chapter 34

Emily wandered thoughtfully through the trees. *It really was beautiful in here, in a creepy sort of way.* Trees hugged up against each other, the green moss wrapping around the trunks of even the dead trees, as if to give the impression the trees were still alive.

She climbed between two trees, letting her yellow ribbon unravel as she went. Looking back, it streamed behind her. *Like a yellow brick road,* she mused. *And ahead … is there an OZ for me?*

The last of her ribbon ran through her fingers. *I guess this is as far as I go.*

Emily looked around. The trees pressed in close here. One humped over another, the roots and trunks twisted together. She saw one bent trunk and sat down on the lap of the tree.

Her heart was racing. She took out Josh's picture and unfolded it. He'd drawn the two of them together, holding each other. Their bodies pressed together, fitting like two puzzle pieces, as they looked at each other. She sighed.

Why couldn't they have found each other years ago? Why now when all she wanted to do was go to sleep and not have to deal with lost, found and lost twins, with mothers dying and... and.

Emily took the bottle of pain pills out of her pack, took the cap off her water bottle and quickly swallowed three pills. Putting them down for the time being, she looked at the drawing again.

Dear, sweet Josh. Sure, he was about as messed up as she was, but he'd listened to her. He'd seen her. Thinking about that, Emily reached down into her pack, took her compact out, and opened it.

Looking her reflection, Emily thought about the mirrors in her dream and the mirrors in the train station. *Well, I can see myself at least. I'm still here.* She shoved her hair back out of her face. *I can take care of that,* she thought and swigged down several more of the Ty-4s. Still looking in the mirror, she thought about Jinn. *In the dream, Jinn told me she didn't want to die. She jumped out of airplanes and jumped off cliffs, but she didn't want to die. But she did. I so wish she hadn't.*

Emily sat up straighter, dropping the compact into the dense undergrowth, where it caught the one beam of sun that found its way through the thickly leaved canopy overhead.

Why did I think that? So she'd be here and I wouldn't? That makes no sense. I want us both here, but she's dead. I found her only to lose her.

Emily slid off the bent tree and leaned against it. *I lose everyone I love. I lost Grandma Alice. I lost mom. I lost my baby. I lost Jinn just when I found her…I've lost Josh just when I found someone I could really love. No. I can't love Josh. I just met him. Yet I let every terrible thought about Jinn go the second she took my hand. I love her. Can I love him?*

Almost as if sampling a box of chocolates, Emily swallowed three more pills. She swiped her hand across her mouth.

A movement caught her eye and she looked over to see a large blue butterfly balanced on a thin stem. It opened its wings and held them there, before flittering up, past her and then around a tree.

I'm glad there are pretty things here. I wonder where Minami is. She wanted us to come here, wanted me to come here, so, I am here sitting all alone in the forest of trees trying to find the meaning of life.

She shook her head and everything went blurry for a moment. *Pills must be working. Where was I? Oh. Minami.*

"Emily."

She looked up to see Minami floating where the butterfly had been.

"There you are. So. I came to Aokigahara, just as you wanted. Was there supposed to be some grand revelation here or something?"

"That's entirely up to you. You can die here. I have no power to stop you."

Emily shook her head. "I have to die here, die now. I remember my mother always complaining I never finished anything I started."

"Have you ever thought there might have been very good reasons that you didn't finish things? Isn't it true that sometimes being halfway through something is precisely where you were meant to go and that, being at that halfway point, you learned what you needed to know, thereby also finding out that you needn't go further down that specific path?"

Emily blinked her eyes hard. She was having trouble focusing on Minami. "You are confusing me."

"What do you want to do, Emily? Really, really want to do?"

"I want to find Josh," she said without thinking.

"Why?"

"Because I think I'm in love with him and … and," her voice trailed off.

"Remember, whether or not you choose to kill yourself here, Emily, it is your choice. You can choose to die. Or, you can choose to live. Jinn didn't have that choice. You do. Choose well."

"But it is more than just Josh. I've lost everything I've ever loved. I'd probably just lose Josh, too," she paused, a scared look crossing her features, "if I haven't already."

"That remains your choice. The one thing about losing those whom you cared for is that, now, there is no one left to criticize your choices and the only one who has to abide by them is you. What do you choose?" The flames floating on either side of Minami flashed iridescent blue for a moment and then blinked out. "I can stay here no longer, Emily. I pray you choose well the path that is right for you." With those words, Minami was gone.

Emily tried to think about what Minami had said. It was so hard to think. *Why is it so hard to think? Oh. The pills.*

With a flash of insight, Emily had several thoughts instantaneously. She leaned over and put her finger halfway down her throat until she vomited up the pills she had taken. She drank some more water and then forced herself to throw up again.

She knew what she needed to do. She knew what she wanted to do and *it wasn't to die in this god-forsaken forest!*

Emily took off running, following the bright flash of yellow through the trees. She leapt over fallen branches, climbed between massive rocks and ran. She realized she was almost back to the path when her foot went down into a hole. She wrenched it horribly as her forward movement caused her to fall, twisting it further.

She tried to pull it out, but it was stuck. *No! No. Not now. I have to get to Josh before...*she pulled, grasping at moldering bark and clinging moss, *I have to get to Josh. He can't die. I have to get to him before he ..."*

Tears overflowing her eyes, she tugged and then tugged again. She could not get her foot out.

She pulled and pulled. She felt her shoe come off, heard something far, far away but the forest pressed down on the sound, suffocating it...and she laid her head down on her arm and wept.

I am so tired, she thought. *I'll just rest here for a moment.* Then she thought she heard the sound again. *It can't be Josh, can it?"*

Taking a deep breath, Emily screamed Josh's name as loudly as she could. At the same time, she pulled hard again. Her foot slid, bleeding and bruised, out of the ancient lava tube. Standing, she yelped as she realized she couldn't put any weight on it at all.

Looking around, she found a broken branch and used it to help support her weight. She hopped and slid her way between the trees. Suddenly she realized she'd lost the yellow ribbon. Scared, she spun around, but couldn't see it anywhere and now she was so tangled up, she didn't even know which way to go.

Looking around wildly, she saw a rock that she though looked familiar and headed towards it. "Josh!" she screamed again. She had to find the trail and then follow his red ribbon. Emily tripped over a root buried in moss and fell hard. She landed on a small hillock covered in moss, but her head grazed a hidden rock as she fell. *Smells good,* she thought. *Smells so good. I'll just wait for him here,* and, with that thought, unconsciousness overcame her.

Chapter 35

Josh made it back to the path, found Emily's yellow ribbon and started picking his way through the trees to follow it. The trees were taller here and growing closely together. As much as he wanted to flat out sprint, it was impossible to run at all. At one point, she had circled back only a few trees down from where she had squeezed between two trees and a huge moss encrusted boulder. There was no way Josh could fit between them and he had to circle back.

He was thinking that he had to be getting to the end of her ribbon, when he thought he heard someone cry out. He stopped and listened. Shaking his head, he figured that it couldn't have been Emily because it came from behind him somewhere. He continued on, climbing over two large rocks and squeezing underneath a tree so twisted it looked like it had grown around itself.

Then he heard something again. Again, it sounded as if it was behind him and off to the left. *It sounded like his name. It had to be Emily, but where was she?* He turned around, almost willing her to cry out again.

"Emily," he yelled. "Em? Answer me!" Only a deathly silence answered him. Deciding he should continue following her ribbon, he saw a place where it looked like someone had fallen. Looking closely at the ground, he could see when it looked as if that person had veered off and away from the ribbon. *What do I do? Follow the slight marks on the ground or…?*

Deciding to take a chance, he tore off a piece of his t-shirt, tied it to a branch and continued, almost crawling along, to follow the marks on the ground. It didn't look like footprints, but instead as if something had dragged here recently.

Stopping again to tie another piece of his shirt to a branch, he then continued crawling along. Losing all marks for a minute, he stood and climbed up and over a pile of black boulders. A flash of something yellow caught his eye, and he thought he'd found her ribbon again. When he came closer, he saw Emily lying in a bed of moss as if she were asleep.

Panic sent adrenaline surging through him; he covered the distance to Emily in a heartbeat. "Emily. Emily, wake up."

When she didn't respond, he moved around her, noticing as he did, that she'd lost her shoe and that her foot was bruised and swollen. There was blood matting the hair on one side of her head as well. He felt for her pulse and felt it beating strongly.

She was still alive. "Emily, c'mon now. Wake up, Em. It's me, Josh. Oh Em, you *have* to wake up!"

She moved slightly, and then her eyes fluttered open. "Josh? Oh, I *knew* you'd find me." She smiled weakly. "My head hurts."

Although he'd heard her comment about her head, he was still stuck on the fact that she'd said she knew he'd find her.

"You *knew* I'd find you?" he asked.

"Uh huh. I tried to get to you. I didn't want you to die without knowing…"

"Without knowing what?"

"That I love you. I know I said I knew you'd find me, but what made you come after me?"

He smiled. "Because I couldn't let you die without knowing that I loved you too!"

She reached for him, but he backed away a bit. "Before any of that, what happened to your foot and your head?"

"I got my foot stuck in a hole and ended up using that stick as a crutch," she pointed, "and then I tripped and landed here. I think I hit my head on the rock." She put her hand to the side of her head. "Owww. It hurts."

Looking at her eyes, Josh was relieved to see that her pupils were the same size. "I think you'll be okay. Good thing you were using that stick," he said. "It's how I found you. I followed the tracks you made with the stick!"

"The important thing is that you were looking for me and found me," she said happily, as she struggled to sit up. As she did, her head swam.

As she swayed, Josh knelt to support her. "Guess I didn't throw up all of the Ty-4s."

"You took them? All of them?" Now Josh was scared all over again.

"No, I'd only taken about ten before I started thinking straight. Minami came," she finished.

"I saw her too, and then she suddenly left. Maybe she came to you."

"Maybe she did," Emily smiled. "I guess my headache should go away soon," she giggled, "after the Tylenol. Oh Josh, what were we thinking?"

"I was thinking just as I have for months. I wasn't taking into consideration all the changes that happened on our journey. The biggest change is you, Em. Somehow you've changed my perspective."

"Should a voice beyond the trees start singing, 'I can see clearly now?' " she asked with a smile.

"Absolutely not. Last thing I need now is to think I'm going crazy!" he said firmly before sweeping her into his arms and kissing her. When Emily came up for air a few minutes later, she leaned back so she could look at him.

"We still have lots of talking to do, you know. We are both still fairly screwed up."

"But not, I think, as badly as we were before."

"We'll muddle through it—"

"Together," he answered with a smile. And that was just it. They'd work through things together.

"Let's get you up so we can get out of here. We only have a few hours until dark."

"I don't think I could have stood being here at night."

"Me neither," he answered.

With Emily leaning heavily on Josh, and using the stick as a crutch, they haltingly made their way back to the main path. The going was easier there, and soon they were where the old woman's ribbon cut off through the trees.

"Do you think we should … ?" Emily began.

"Try and find her? Are you up for it?"

"I can't stand the thought that, if we don't, we'll never know."

"Okay then."

Not even five minutes later, Emily let out a high squeak. Up ahead of them, the old woman hung limply from a rope tied to a branch. Clearly dead, her body turned slowly back and forth.

Emily leaned over suddenly and lost whatever medication was still in her stomach.

"Should we leave her like that, or should we get her down?"

"Josh, we need to get her down. It is just too sad to leave her like that. That poor, old, sad woman."

Josh climbed the short way up into the tree and untied the knot holding the rope to the branch. He tried to lower her gently, but she still landed hard. "I am surprised the knot held, or that the branch didn't break under her weight."

"Me too," murmured Emily as she arranged the woman into a more dignified position. She took off her now soiled jacket and laid it over the woman's face. Looking around, she saw some of the tiny blue flowers that were everywhere in the forest. "Josh," she asked, "would you pick some of those for me, please?"

When he had, Emily arranged them in a small bouquet and placed them within the woman's gnarled hands. She said a prayer, and then standing, limped over to Josh.

"Guess that's the best we can do," she said softly. Together the two made their way back to the trail and stated walking out.

Behind them, they never saw Minami watching them, nor the two ribbons of silver tears streaking down her face.

Just before they exited the path on to the main path... they looked up and saw Minami floating before them.

"That was a nice thing you did back there."

"We had to do something," Emily responded.

"Still, it was a very caring thing to do for someone you didn't know. She was my twin sister," Minami continued.

"But you're so young and she was really old," commented Josh.

"I look as I looked the day she killed me."

"What?" Josh sputtered.

"Emily will tell you all about it. Things have come full circle now and at long last, I am free to go."

Minami was now only a pale, almost translucent version of herself. "I was finally able to forgive her. This journey was one for all of us, although I didn't know that at the beginning."

She looked down at Josh and Emily, standing together, hand in hand. With the last bit of her self, she peered into Emily, and then smiled at the twin beginnings of life she saw.

"Continue to choose well..." With that last instruction, Minami's essence rose in multicolored ribbons of light – until she disappeared into the sunset.

Unpacking ~ AN EPILOGUE

Three years later

Josh looked up over his easel to watch his twins sleep in the arbor in the back yard. Curled up between them was Grandma Alice's cat Sherry.

Alice Minami and Emma Jinn had arrived a little over eight and a half months after they'd returned from Japan. Josh had given up his apartment, Emily had sold her house, and they were now living in a house up in the hills above San Francisco. He and Em had opened their own art gallery featuring his artwork and her photography, along with work from other local artists. The tourists seemed to like their work, and Josh and Emily enjoyed running the gallery together.

They were both still in counseling. Josh had found a doctor who had diagnosed him as being borderline bi-polar along with his having ADHD – both of which had been the roots of his problem all along. The new doctor had figured out that Josh had been on multiple medications from several doctors that all had had a possible side effect of causing suicidal thoughts. Taken together, the medications raised the suicidal tendencies or side effects exponentially. Now, on medications that worked together and did not have those side effects, Josh was able to think and react in a far more positive manner. On Emily's side of things, a little medication, the counseling they both attended, and the knowing she was loved had truly helped. They were happy, healthy and an excellent balance for each other. *Like complimentary colors,* he mused.

He tapped the end of his paintbrush against his bottom teeth. Emily should be back soon, he thought. She'd had several errands this morning and had wanted to stop in the gallery to check on some recent sales. They'd never, nor would they ever sell the painting they'd retrieved from Jinn's apartment. It hung opposite the doorway to the gallery. He liked thinking of it being the first thing people saw upon entering the gallery. It always made him smile.

Josh looked down at the painting of his sleeping children. They had all lived on: Alice, Minami, Emma and the Jinn she became. "I think I will name this one, *Tomorrows,*" he said softly.

"You might find your tomorrows a bit more crowded, dear heart," said Emily coming up behind him. "We're pregnant again!"

"We are?" Josh dropped his paintbrush as he grabbed Em in a hug and swung her around. Holding her, he kissed the tip of her nose before asking, "When?"

"In about six months. "

"Is it a girl or a boy?"

"I don't know yet, silly. Any preferences?"

"Healthy!"

"Josh, I have a great name for the baby either way, girl or boy."

"What?"

"Journey," she smiled.

"Perfect choice," he said. "I have some news too, although it pales in comparison to your announcement," he smiled broadly at her. "I completed the poem that will go with the painting I finished last week."

"You mean the 'light beam' one of the forest?"

"Yes, I've named the painting *Minami Dreams.* The poem is on my desk.

The twins, awakened from their nap, ran to hug their mother. Leaving her husband to work on his current piece of art, Emily and the twins walked to the kitchen door and went inside. While the kids munched on some apple slices at the table, Emily slipped into the office. She picked up the handwritten sheet of paper lying on the desk ...

Aokigahara Jukai

Honshu Island King,
Mt Fuji guards the entrance:
Forest of the Damned.
Sleeping at the foot of a Japanese volcano
ancient forest of convoluted trees,
knees bent up, like benches,
but there are few who care to sit.
They who journey here seek eternal sleep.

Midst sleeping trees,
Aokigahara waits:
She knows they will come.

Train station lined with mirrors
to remind travelers that they can, indeed, be seen:
they are not, yet, the invisible ones.
The intent journey from across the waters to seek
their own redemption, lose themselves
in evergreen and beech trees
whose roots gnarl above
the volcanic ground, obscuring hidden caves.

Buy your ribbons –
bread crumbs should you change
your mind; opt to live.

Called Black Sea of Trees,
sunlight does not penetrate,
leaving the wanderer, in darkness.
Apollo butterflies glow in the shadows,

but only rarely does
the song of bird burst forth.

They say that the souls
of the dead linger here.
White draped Yurei waft
through rope tied boughs where the
dead hang in mid scream.

Here, it is the hempen way,
others seek a golden bridge,
a short flight to drowning
in the uneasy waters of the bay.

Signs at the entrance to the forest
urge rethinking,
but the majority are past reading,
care not for warnings nor turning back.

They leave their pretty ribbons behind
to flutter in the breeze,
enticing others to follow.

Along the way, they who go to die
shed their belongings:
wallets scavenged by the living,
moldering photographs,
and pairs of glasses:
who wants to see what lies ahead?

Still. The essence of Aokigahara,
the somber beauty
of the forest at Mt Fuji's feet
sends out its siren's call.

It heeds no boundary,
for it is where the border
is but a gauzy wisp of dreams
on the Journey to Jukai.

There are answers
in Aokigahara:
but the dead will not answer
and the living no longer question.

IF YOU ARE IN CRISIS,
please call 1-800-273-TALK (8255).